He reached out for the notep_____
began to list items that might be _____
if, everything tallied he might star_____ ___ ___e
likelihood that a human voice could be _____ and
enhanced enough to make it, effectively, the_____ce of
charismatic appeal. A George Whitefield voice; a Bryan
voice. Perhaps even a Judy Garland voice, begging only
for love.

Or an Adolf Hitler voice, commanding hate.

Dieter Mainz, Innsbruck; daughter? he wrote.

German electronics advances 1930, he added.

And *Goering—Reichstag tunnel,* and *Hess flight,* and
Shirer quote, and finally *Kalvin bio.* This last item would
be in NBN files and was as simple a matter as patching
the modem in his study into NBN's computer.

But if, by some tremendous long shot, this tale had any
substance, then the government's own electronic ears might
be alert for anyone who became curious about Walter
Kalvin. How much power could a White House
administrator assemble in six months; enough to set
requirements for NSA and CIA? Not unless he had the
obedient help of the President of the United States.

A vagrant tagline tugged at his mind: *The paranoids
are out to get me. . . .*

"Christ, it's catching," he muttered aloud, and reached
for the phone.

—from *Silent Thunder* by Dean Ing

"Has the reader hanging on to each page!"

—Associated Press on Dean Ing's
The Ransom of Black Stealth One

DEAN ING
—SILENT—
THUNDER

ROBERT A.
HEINLEIN
UNIVERSE

A TOM DOHERTY ASSOCIATES BOOK
NEW YORK

Tor SF Double No. 31

SILENT THUNDER

UNIVERSE

A Tor Book
Published by Tom Doherty Associates, Inc.
49 West 24th Street
New York, N.Y. 10010

Cover art by Joe DeVito

ISBN: 0-812-50265-5

First edition: July 1991

Printed in the United States of America

0 9 8 7 6 5 4 3 2 1

SILENT THUNDER
by Dean Ing

For the brain trust:
Tim, Tim, Ev, and Joe.

ONE

March, 1967

ONLY A MAN DESTINED FOR GREATNESS, SERGEANT WALter Kalvin reflected, could keep his alertness up and his temper down on a night as cheerless as this. Even with mature chestnut trees for a windbreak in the gloom of the *Stadtpark*, Vienna's night wind could bite like a Doberman. The major stood slope-shouldered under his heavy European overcoat, with his furled umbrella hooked into a coat pocket. He had emptied his own packet of Pall Malls an hour before and was smoking one of Kalvin's Salems now, cursing the menthol in his lungs, the Viennese slush under his feet, and the man who might or might not contact the Americans as promised. *He likes his vices unmentholated,* Kalvin told himself, drawing some comfort from the major's inferior showing. Competitiveness had been part of Walter Kalvin's legacy from immigrant parents. *If I had oak leaves instead of four lousy stripes, I could tell this guy to go buy himself some Austrian cigarettes. Well, some day. . . .*

Neither man wore military insignia, though both carried
Air Force ID. While civilian clothes of European cut did
not assure freedom from surveillance, American uniforms
would have drawn more attention than a bonfire in the
Stadtpark's deepest shadows. Their flat little German-
made, nine-millimeter automatics in shoulder holsters were
government issue. Though he had been reposted to Air
Force Intelligence for less than a year, after someone noticed his fluency in German, Walter Kalvin had heard his
share of stories about Vienna during his familiarization
with the pistol. A man who looked out of place in Central
Europe might pick up a half-dozen tails: one KGB, one
CIA, and four free-lancers who made precarious livings
by selling tidbits to all sides. The free-lancers, it was said,
rarely carried firearms. As the joke went, cloaks were out
but daggers were definitely in.

This was Sergeant Kalvin's fifth field sortie from the air
base near Wiesbaden, but his first into Austria. He had
drawn this duty only because the major did not speak German. And Dieter Mainz, the man who had made contact
with a regular Air Force officer leading by stages to this
peculiar rendezvous, had claimed to speak no English.
Kalvin knew that the job should have been taken over by
the CIA, but it seemed barely possible that Dieter Mainz
could advance a few careers in Air Force Intelligence. At
the moment, Kalvin did not dream that it would advance
him far beyond a military commission. Mainz was just a
contact, though a peculiar one from the start.

According to the case file, 'Dieter Mainz' was probably
a beard, a false name. The real Mainz, an audio engineer
with the prewar *Reichs Rundfunk* group in Berlin, had disappeared on the Night of the Long Knives in 1934. Mainz
had been one of the many victims of Hitler's first great
domestic massacre. To young Walter Kalvin it was the
stuff of legend, a web of events that had spun out their

courses before he was old enough to read. If the man had not resurfaced in over thirty years, in all likelihood he was long dead. Still, if they failed to make contact on this bitter night, Kalvin and the major would have to try again in seven days.

The major stamped his feet and grunted in pain, the umbrella a ludicrous pendulum at his side. "Goddammit, sergeant, any man who's two hours late is a man who is not going to show!"

"Yes, sir," said Kalvin. Then, more softly: "Should you be mentioning rank out here?"

The major, who tended to be lax about professionalism but knew very well when it was called into question, stared hard at Kalvin. "Is that insubordination?"

"No, sir," said Kalvin. At that instant he saw a two-legged shadow crossing from a footpath in the distance, a slender silhouette that caused distant lights to wink as it approached. In low tones Kalvin added, "This could be our man."

To his credit, the major had seen it too. Mainz had been very specific, insisting on his own recognition signals. The major grabbed his umbrella, slung its furled length over one shoulder like a hunting rifle, and walked slowly forward with Kalvin beside him. The shadow began to resolve itself into a man of slight stature, hands in the pockets of his greatcoat, hatbrim hiding his face. When they were ten paces apart, Kalvin began to talk conversationally but in German. The major swung the umbrella to his other shoulder according to plan, nodding as if he understood Kalvin.

"Herr Donner," said the man facing them, and stopped. It was a common surname.

"Herr Sprache," Kalvin responded with an unlikely surname. Together, the names formed a key word. As tradecraft it was dreadfully amateurish, but Mainz had

called the shots. *Donnersprache*, thunderspeak, was still
among the unsolved mysteries of Hitler's Reich. According
to the best guesses of spook historians, Donnersprache
had pertained to electronics, probably an aid to eaves-
dropping, no doubt primitive by modern standards but still
an enigma. No mention of it had ever been found in official records, though the two men closest to Adolf Hitler
had at various times scribbled cryptic references to the
thing, or possibly the person, called Donnersprache.

A hand came out of the greatcoat, wearing a glove, and
the Americans shook it. Rapidly, in German, Kalvin explained that the gentleman beside him did not speak the
language. Was it possible for them to continue their discussion while riding in a BMW sedan with an excellent
heater?

"Naturlich," of course, Mainz replied. "But permit me
to retrieve a traveling bag I left among the bushes nearby."
Later, Kalvin would report the old man's age as nearing
eighty, his speech halting and sometimes vague as might
befit a man whose mind had begun to fail. Kalvin's true
impression was that this preternaturally alert little gnome
of a man kept all his mental bricks neatly stacked.

The major clearly loathed his role but accepted it anyway, hurrying off to retrieve their rented BMW as the old
man half-trotted back to the shadows of anonymous shrub-
bery. Waiting alone for the car near the *Rechte Bahngasse*,
Kalvin felt that the old man had still not decided to trust
the Americans. One or both of those coat pockets, he
judged, was full of handgun—an infraction far more serious in Austria than in, say, the United States. For Kalvin
and the major, sidearms were more acceptable; above a
certain level of business such things were taken for
granted.

Dieter Mainz returned before the major did, lugging an
old leather valise that, Kalvin presumed, held the secrets
of Donnersprache. Kalvin tried not to stare at it, smiling

instead at his companion, who kept jerking his head away from the street to scan the shadows. "I think you need not fear for your life," Kalvin said, noticing the old man's nervous glances. "How important can Donnersprache be, in a time when a radio transmitter can be hidden in the heel of a shoe?"

"Can that transmitter hypnotize ten million listeners?"

Kalvin shrugged. "I suppose it depends on what is said," he hedged, watching a bulky shadow stroll into the street two hundred meters away. He tensed as the distant stranger began to walk in their direction. *This old guy is getting to me,* he admitted to himself.

"No, it does not matter what is said when the machine makes one's words seem absolutely true. What matters is the listener's capacity, and desire, to believe in something." Mainz said it dogmatically, as if lecturing on fundamentals.

Before enlisting to avoid the draft and a rifleman's fate in Vietnam, Walter Kalvin had been a mediocre student of rhetoric at NYU. The concept of charisma, the overwhelming power of certain individuals to convince many others, had never seemed so real to him as it did at this moment. *Maybe old Mainz himself has charisma,* thought Kalvin. *He's sure got my nerves twanging. Lord, what if it's a kind of force field, and he has one in his pocket?* Chuckling at his own fanciful notion, Kalvin said, "Perhaps you will tell me exactly what Donnersprache is, and what it does. Do you have it with you, Herr Mainz?"

"I should not be offering to sell the machine to a man who does not already know such basic things," Mainz protested. "The Bolsheviks know that much, at least."

The major was taking an infernally long time, and it seemed to Kalvin that the old man was rethinking his decision. To keep him engaged, Kalvin asked, "How can you be certain the Russians know something I don't?"

"Because they have no other reason to ensure that poor,

addled Rudolf Hess rots alone in Spandau Prison,'' the old man said.

The man walking toward them seemed to loom, now, though he was a hundred paces away. "I don't understand," said Kalvin, reaching into his coat for his Salems, caressing the butt of the pistol for added confidence. He decided he did not need the cigarette.

A sigh. "Last October, the Nazi criminals in Spandau were released; von Schirach and Speer," the old man went on. "All but Hess, whom everyone knows has lost his mind. But even a crazy man can make sense at times. That is what the Bolsheviks fear. Schirach was a fool, and Speer only a hapless architect. If that swine Hitler would not trust his own Gestapo with Donnersprache, why would he entrust its secrets to such as those? No; only a few knew. Those of us who developed it, and of course Goering—and Hess.''

Sergeant Walter Kalvin began to feel as if he was floundering in a nightmare, one dreamed many times before but only partly remembered. This old German was rattling off the names of men who had produced and directed the most savage war in human history. It was true, Speer and Schirach had recently been freed from Spandau to great hubbub in the German press. Now, jailers of four nations continued to operate the castle-like Spandau Prison for a solitary inmate: Rudolf Hess. Three of those nations claimed that they would be happy to release Hess, a man they did not regard as a war criminal. Only the Soviet Union insisted that Hess remain imprisoned in that vast pile of stone on the outskirts of Berlin without possibility of parole. To Kalvin, the issue had never seemed very important until now.

Was it imagination, or was the hulking stranger walking more slowly? Gazing at the face of Dieter Mainz, Kalvin asked his question softly: "Can Donnersprache be that important today?''

For the first time, Mainz turned to scan Kalvin's face at

close range, and in the lined old face Kalvin thought he could read utter despair. "You would not ask," he said slowly, "if you had seen its effect on an audience. Perhaps you are immune; some are. Some more, some less."

Kalvin's chill had become internal by now. "I'd like to see this gadget," he said. "Does it still work?"

"No. Only a vacuum tube, I suspect, but the case is—you would say, boob-trap? To open it conventionally is to blow it, and yourself, to pieces." Now, headlights swept across them, high beams flicking twice, the moan of the BMW a familiar voice to Kalvin, who took the old man's arm and stepped toward the street.

But someone did not want them in that car. The big stranger was no longer strolling, but running forward now, holding a small device to his mouth with one hand as he fumbled in his coat with the other.

As the major sizzled past the running man, he must have seen Kalvin draw his pistol. He made the right move, swerving onto the walkway as he braked heavily so that the running man caromed off the right front fender. The man fell hard, cursing in a language Kalvin did not recognize, and came up sitting ten feet from Kalvin, a silenced handgun in his right hand.

The major was shouting, leaning over to fling the front passenger door wide, and Kalvin took two steps as if adjusting his paces for a field goal before he kicked the man's weapon in an arc that sent it spinning far into the darkness.

Kalvin heard a sound like a fist striking a melon, and old Dieter Mainz collided with him from behind. "Get in, get in," he snapped to Mainz, aiming his pistol at the prostrate stranger. At the instant Mainz fell into the front seat, the BMW windshield resounded with an impact that left a hole in its center. Kalvin fought to open the locked rear door, and he saw the yellow wink from a distant line of shrubs a split second before a portion of the windshield imploded, the major's torso slamming back into the seat. The BMW engine began to roar, impotent.

Kalvin raced around the car, hearing another impact as he squatted to open the driver's door, and with the help of Mainz he somehow managed to thrust the major's body aside enough to huddle low at the controls.

They hurtled away in the damaged car, Kalvin obeying the curt instructions of Mainz as he turned this way and that. Once over the Donau Canal, Kalvin turned onto the *Praterstrasse*. "No one is following us," he said, blinking in the breeze through the ruined windshield. To his amazement, the BMW had not yet attracted the *polizei*.

"The gentleman is dead," Mainz replied, and coughed. "Soon, I shall be."

"I got you this far," Kalvin seethed, trying to recall the telephone number he must call only in a situation like this.

"They shot me, you fool," Mainz said. "Someone hidden in the park."

"No, they wouldn't work alone," Kalvin thought aloud. "I'll get you to a hosp—"

"Quiet, let me talk," said Dieter Mainz with soft urgency. "The decision has been made for me. Have you a recorder?"

"Try the major's pockets," Kalvin said. "You must tell me where the nearest hospital is."

Mainz told him, coughing occasionally, fumbling with the little tape recorder until Kalvin punched the right button for him. Mainz spoke for perhaps three minutes before he began to labor for breath, describing a concrete storm drainage sump on the outskirts of Innsbruck, and how a man assuredly would be crushed to death if he failed to observe certain precautions as he climbed down below the grating. The old man began, then, to talk about Donnersprache, and the ways it had been used to weld Germany into a monolith of hatred. Past a certain point of unified public opinion, Mainz was saying, it was no longer a necessary. . . . Mainz left that sentence forever unfinished. Kalvin did not know Mainz was dead until he saw the staring eyes and felt for a pulse.

Accompanied by two dead men in a BMW that featured several obvious bullet holes, Walter Kalvin parked in shadows and made the necessary telephone call. While waiting for help, he hefted the old man's leather bag. It seemed very light, its contents soft, and its brass hasp came loose while Kalvin was handling it. Since the thing had not blown up then, Kalvin checked inside.

It held a change of clothes and a passport. No device with radio tubes, not even a schematic drawing.

Kalvin thought about charisma while he replayed the last testament of Dieter Mainz. Then he replayed it again, starting to hope that the damage assessment team would take its time. Sergeant Walter Kalvin knew, now, where the last surviving Donnersprache device lay hidden. Incredibly, the city of Innsbruck was near enough to his father's beloved Tirol that Kalvin's own accent might go unremarked there. Using the gloves of Dieter Mainz, Kalvin found spare tapes in the major's coat, exchanged the used tape, and wiped the recorder down with great care before cupping the major's dead hand around it. With one gloved hand, he inserted the recorder back into the major's coat. If anyone doubted his initial story, Kalvin knew, he was destined for the tribulations of a lifetime.

If no one did, and if he managed a vacation as far as Innsbruck—and if the last living act of Dieter Mainz was not merely the fantasy of an old man—then Walter Kalvin was destined for greatness.

TWO

May, 1997

THE WATER WAS CLEAR AND NUMBINGLY COLD, MOST OF
it fresh runoff from the snow that still clung to peaks of
Wyoming's Absaroka Range. Secretary Bowden let one of
his matched pair of State Department men hold his boron
fiber flyrod as he began to tighten the straps of his chest-
high waders. Very spendy waders, the latest mid-nineties
technology. Very spendy bodyguards as well, both dressed
for fly-fishing in clothes similar to the secretary's. *Nothing's
too good for the Secretary of State,* Bowden thought, *except
being allowed to do my job.*

"I wouldn't, Mr. Secretary," said his third companion,
a dark, wiry national parks man named Martin. "Keep
the straps loose enough that you could get out of those
waders in a hurry."

Bowden's glance was more quizzical than irked. Most
of his trout fishing had been done from powerboats in
tame lakes while politicking for Harrison Rand's candi-
dacies over the years, so these waders were a new expe-

rience for Bowden. Kenneth Bowden had selected this out-
ing, in part, because he felt deeply in need of some kind
of experience that took little thought, and no politicking.
And for another reason, too, a contact who had not yet
surfaced. . . .

Martin, whose coloring and high cheekbones suggested
he might be part American Indian, went on, "The Yellowstone's not much over crotch deep here, gents, but it has
a stiff current and the rocks are rounded. If those waders
fill with water, you'll want to shuck them in a hurry."

The senior agent frowned. "In three feet of water?"

"People drown," Martin shrugged to the agent. "But
not with me beside them. Anyway, that's where the lun-
kers are, out there in the current. Of course I'll go first.
Part of my job," he added.

The younger agent sighed audibly and stared at his hik-
ing boots. "I'll go," he said.

Bowden waved the men away. "No. Martin's dressed
for it, gentlemen, and I promise we won't go more than
fifty feet out."

They didn't like it, but they permitted it, moving down-
stream at Martin's suggestion. If Bowden went under, his
bodyguards would already be in position to scramble for
a rescue. This was Bowden's first three-day vacation since
Congress had voted to accept him as Harrison Rand's Secretary of State, and he was tiring of it before he'd even
tied into his first trout. Bowden knew he had become physically soft, and at age sixty he did not want to feel ashamed
to grip Martin's shoulder as they edged out, feeling the
tug of the Yellowstone River.

Nonetheless, he felt shame. *Just one more little re-
minder of impotence on top of all the rest,* he admitted to
himself. *My God, I haven't even made it with Lucille in
over a month.* Bowden wondered if the sex lives of the
Secretaries of Defense and Commerce were suffering as

well. Who would have believed that an outsider like that goddamned Walter Kalvin could usurp so much power, so fast, from the position of White House Chief of Staff?

"Let the river carry your fly," Martin suggested, as Bowden tried a sweeping backcast. The guide stood facing away from shore, his voice barely audible in the white noise of rushing water. "That way we can attend to business."

Bowden glanced around, read Martin's faint smile, and pretended he was still interested in fishing. "What business is that?" he asked.

Without preamble: "I'm your contact, sir. We're convinced that Undersecretary Parker's death was a deliberate hit," Martin said, seeming to study the river. "We're not questioning whether Parker was killed by that mugger: he was. But we've done a careful profile on the mugger, and he'd been a suspect on two previous contract killings. He became an addict, but he wasn't the kind to take a deliberate overdose. Needle mark in his arm was a nasty one, too; maybe the guy was struggling. In any case, he can't give his end of it now that he's safely dead."

"Safe for whom? Richard Parker was a good man. He resigned as a protest on my behalf, Martin. If he wasn't safe, who is?"

"Everyone at cabinet level, we think, so long as they don't step out of the game."

Now, Bowden drew in slack line and glanced at Martin as he made another leisurely cast. "You mean, if I should resign, I might wind up like poor Dick Parker?"

"Any member of President Rand's cabinet who walks out complaining that he's a rubber stamp for Walter Kalvin could wind up on a slab, sir. I wouldn't tempt fate by trying it if I were you. Just hang in there. These things take time."

"Whose time is it taking? All I have from you people is a handshake and a promise," Bowden said.

"That handshake's been good enough for centuries," Martin replied. "If it makes you feel any better, this little meeting is expensive for me; it's my last day as Cody Martin, and I'd got to where I liked it here. I was DIA for twelve years before I became a sacrificial lamb."

The Defense Intelligence Agency was an arm of the Defense Department, therefore not under control of State or Treasury. Bowden made a test connection: "You're telling me Secretary Canales runs your group?"

"No, sir," said Martin; "because he doesn't. Consider us privately funded, and please don't imagine that we're some kind of radical death squad. Where due process is concerned you can think of us as a *life* squad. We've all been professionals in one agency or another. But someone botched the job badly for Mr. Parker. We don't believe in coincidence. Somebody left Mr. Parker unprotected."

"You'd think," Bowden said, "a man in my position would have some muscle of his own he could call on."

"No sir, beyond your Bureau of Intelligence and Research. What I think is, all your men but one could be yours, and you'd still be in trouble. Same with Defense, Treasury, and Interior. It's a bitch," he said, smiling as Bowden turned a vexed glance on him. "That's why I'm here, sir."

Bowden nodded and remembered to wave a thumbs-up toward the men on the riverbank before he tried another cast. "Why haven't you simply gone to the President about the problems with Walt Kalvin?"

"Why haven't *you*, Mr. Secretary?"

Bowden's laugh was short and mirthless. "Good point. We don't know what else Dick Parker was hinting about to the press, and he didn't see fit to confide in me with it. First damned thing Harry Rand would do is call good old Walt Kalvin in and ask him."

"Exactly." Both men glanced across the shallow river as another fisherman played a hefty trout. "Better reel in and let me change flies, Mr. Secretary. It could look odd if you don't get a strike."

"By God, that's right," Bowden said. "Why haven't I?"

"Something I smeared on the fly," Martin said, and laughed as Bowden cursed. "Figured we needed to concentrate on business."

Martin selected a fat black-and-yellow fly from the assortment stuck into his shapeless hat as Bowden retrieved the end of his line. "This McGinty should get you some action, sir."

"So far I haven't heard what other kind of action I can expect," Bowden said.

"You may not believe this, sir, but we really do believe in the system. I was told to ask you for a decision. Because of Mr. Parker, it's your decision—and whatever you say, believe me, we will do."

"That smacks of power I'm not sure I want, but ask away," Bowden said, holding a scarlet and black Royal Coachman fly that seemed suspiciously oily and, even after its dunking, exuded an unpleasant musk.

"Mr. Parker was a computer hacker; a hobby of his," said Martin, running the loop of the new fly onto monofilament leader. "If he had anything on Kalvin that was important enough to get him offed, he just might have put it into his private disk files."

"Surely they've been collected," Bowden exclaimed.

"Not from his girlfriend's apartment."

Bowden stared. "Dick Parker was a model husband! We had him checked six ways from Saturday, Martin, and he wasn't into hanky-panky."

"He was into an old classmate, is what he was into," Martin said, releasing the McGinty as if he expected it to fly away of its own volition. "Good friend of long standing; she just didn't remain standing when he visited her apartment. Actually, he sometimes went there without her,

THREE

ALAN RAMSAY SHOULDERED HIS WAY THROUGH THE FRONT
door of his Hyattsville apartment on a muggy Thursday
evening carrying two armloads of groceries, a mouthful
of keycards, a handful of personal mail, and a letter bomb
in a manila envelope. The envelope contained no percus-
sion snapper or thin sheet of hexyl explosive; only words
that were to detonate Ramsay's life into smouldering fragments.

He made coffee in his usual manner, the way he'd
learned in the jock dorm back in Lincoln, Nebraska,
twenty years ago. Right arm snakes out to the dregs container while left hand twists the faucet handle; lean to the
left and haul in a fresh dollop of coffee grounds while the
right hand raps the container to dump the old dregs; quick
double-handed rinse of the container, three seconds max,
then cross arms. Ladle fresh grounds with *right* hand while
left sweeps Pyrex pot under faucet. A handball champ
named Jacque Flory had coached him in the move that

installed fresh grounds and hit the percolator switch while the pot filled. Flory had owned the Cornhusker record for coffee setup: thirty-seven seconds flat.

Ramsay whisked the pot across, poured its water into the machine, set the empty pot in place, wiped his hands on his video-blue shirtfront, and consulted the digital readout on Mister Coffee: almost fifty seconds. Hell, he was getting slower every year. The process still delighted his daughter, Laurie, on nights the kid spent with him. Daddy's trick, she called it. Kathleen had called it macho; claimed it was typical of the million little acts that abraded a marriage to shreds. Alan Ramsay called it second-rate because he would never beat Flory's record.

The truth was that Ramsay had always been driven by self-doubt, the kind of pitiless internal criticism that can drive a man to perform beyond all reason—and then to conclude that he should have done better. If Kathleen left him, then it had to be his fault. If his three-times-a-week calisthenics made him capable of seventy pushups, why, then he had to work up to eighty-five and inflamed tendons. If his craggy good looks and humming vitality made him a popular NBN face on the Washington beat, he promptly began to worry that his value was only cosmetic. And to dig a little harder for a story; keep asking the next question; keep wondering if the answers made sense. NBN had discovered that when Alan Ramsay wondered out loud, from scripts he wrote unaided, thoughtful viewers loved it. Those commentaries were not news, but not quite editorials either. NBN identified them as pages from 'The Ramsay File' and did not worry too much about precisely what category they fitted. They were popular, and that was enough. So long as Ramsay retained his appeal as a thoughtful gadfly, network nabobs could bask in reflected ethics and take Ramsay's cachet to the bank. They paid Ramsay well, though not exorbitantly, and wisely avoided reining him in too much.

He laid the mail out on his kitchen table as if dealing a hand of solitaire, then shoved the bills aside. One evening a week, he devoted an hour to such stuff; and thank God, his influx of forwarded fan mail had nearly ceased two weeks after that 'True Believers' commentary of his on NBN affiliate stations. The downside of feeling your commitment, he had learned, was the impulse to read fan mail and, sometimes, to spend time responding. At age forty-one, Ramsay was starting to count the ticks of life's clock.

While stuffing his refrigerator with groceries—including sticks of string cheese for Laurie and soy cheddar for himself—he made quick guesses about the personal mail. One piece, in a manila, had been forwarded from the Overseas Press Club. That happened perhaps three times a year and usually came from someone with savvy who wanted to avoid the vagaries of a network's internal mail system. Ramsay opened the manila with the short, dull blade of the mail-slitter in his money clip. Kathleen had been leery of weaponlike gadgets, and he'd let this one stay dull, as if he expected Kathleen to return.

Wheels within wheels. The letter inside bore a Baltimore postmark and contained a note on the elegant buff stationery of one Matthew Alden, attorney, and still another envelope with 'Alan Ramsay, NBN' scrawled across it by someone in a terrible hurry.

Alden's cover note was brief. *Dear Mr. Ramsay: I am forwarding the enclosure by request of an acquaintance of long standing whom I shall call Cody Martin. Evidently his letter is his response to your recent video commentary on the influx of so-called 'True Believers' in the new Rand Administration (congratulations, by the way; I saw it). Beyond this, I know nothing of the contents. Mr. Martin made it harrowingly clear that I must not read his letter.*

He also hinted that you might doubt his bona fides. I can attest to his steadiness, his courage as a witness in a string of federal prosecutions some years ago, and his sense of commitment to his country. 'Cody Martin'—his most recent name—was long active in the intelligence community, and his titles changed irregularly. Make what you will of that. I doubt that I ever knew, or ever will know, his real name. In the present matter his concern seemed unusually acute. He is not a man who strains at trifles. Sincerely, Matthew L. Alden.

Ramsay tapped the edge of the envelope against his teeth, fighting the urge to discard it, wondering whether Alden was a real person and, if so, whether he was the dupe of some subtle loony. Washington had more of those per acre than any asylum. Then he sighed and slit the little envelope and unfolded the sheet of paper, with its single spacing on both sides.

Two minutes later, Ramsay dropped the page and vented an almost silent whistle as he stared at the wall above his microwave oven. Then he resumed reading. He then re-read the whole thing slowly while sleet ran along his spine. The paper accentuated the slight tremor of his hands.

At least one assertion, Ramsay had heard as non-news, the kind of fact you edited out unless it became important enough to warrant the ruin of a dead man's reputation. The now-deceased Richard Parker had frequented a woman's Bethesda apartment, motive unknown but presumably not for prayer meetings. That corroboration made it possible for Ramsay to half-believe in an Austrian woman who had, for a price, delivered a copy of her father's recently discovered diary to a State Department aide to Undersecretary Parker. Innsbruck meant little more than skiing to Ramsay, and the name 'Dieter Mainz' meant nothing at all. As the police liked to say, at least it listened; it seemed plausible.

It was the body of the letter that became so wildly implausible that Alan Ramsay could almost see H O A X between the lines. And yet— Walt Kalvin, the incisive chief of Rand's White House staff, had not been born an

American, so under the Constitution he could never run for President. He could, however, help groom a Missouri preacher named Harrison Rand for a senatorial slot and, later, for the race to the White House.

Ramsay also had to admit that there had been scuttlebutt to the effect that Kalvin had been offered a cabinet position. Why had he refused? According to the files of Richard Parker, Kalvin did not want to undergo the kind of scrutiny Congress could bring to bear if he were President Rand's choice for, say, Secretary of State or Interior. In short, Congress could have smirched Kalvin's image. But Congress had no such power over Rand's choice of his Chief of Staff—which was increasingly a crucial position in the White House. Ramsay's 'True Believer' commentary had touched on the dangers of zealots in government, and the zeal with which Kalvin attacked his job. In passing, Ramsay had observed that Walter Kalvin, a zealot without a cabinet position, was becoming Secretary of Everything in the Rand administration.

"He wouldn't have to step down when the President does, either," Ramsay murmured aloud. "No Senate confirmations, no votes to worry about. If succeeding presidents wanted him, Kalvin could hover over the Oval Office as long as he lives. But he'd have to have the devil's own charisma for that. More than Rand himself." Ramsay looked down at the page, not really seeing the print; realizing that if there was any truth to this tale, Walter Kalvin already had the devil's own charisma in something called *Donnersprache*. Maybe that was the source of Rand's personal magnetism, too.

If this Mainz diary could be believed—if indeed a Dieter Mainz had ever existed!—it was possible to add the kind of vibrato and timbre to a voice that brought overwhelming credibility to the speaker. Ramsay cudgeled his memory and came up with two names from Cornhusker rhetoric classes. George Whitefield; William Jennings Bryan. And another which he had heard on old sound tracks: Adolf Hitler. Who was it—yes, randy old Ben Franklin had written about Whitefield, a circuit preacher of modest intellect but with such compelling emotional impact in his voice that most listeners turned out their pockets on the spot—hypnotized, set afire with zeal, utterly convinced of Whitefield's message. Other orators had specifically mentioned their envy of the Whitefield tremolo.

Bryan, a Nebraskan himself, was easy to remember because every schoolkid in the state found the man on their exams. Early in the Twentieth Century, William Jennings Bryan had gained tremendous popular appeal with his oratory: half with the words, half with his great, emotion-laden voice that trembled and fulminated. If the popular vote had counted as much then as it did now, Bryan would have been President. Even then, he damned near made it, despite an intellect that was tepid at best.

The charisma of Adolf Hitler was too well documented to doubt, and anyone who cared to could audit old recordings of the man's fiery oratory. Ramsay's natural skepticism asked it for him: *could it really be that simple?* Was it possible, before 1930, to construct a vacuum tube device capable of taking a man with a strong message and adding overwhelming credibility with enhanced resonance at the right frequencies or filtering of unwanted voice tones?

Well, certainly it would not work on everyone; Parker's notes acknowledged that. The question was whether it had worked on enough people to elect a Missouri senator—or an American president. All you had to do was patch that device into a loudspeaker system. And Walter Kalvin had been Rand's campaign manager.

The notes of Richard Parker, building on this possibly mythical Mainz diary, cited suspicions by German moderates in early 1933 about the loudspeaker system of the Reichstag, the German Parliament building where Hitler had risen to power. It became impossible to check on those suspicions after the fire which leveled the Reichstag in February, 1933, and a tunnel had been found from the Reichstag to the personal home of Hermann Goering.

Mainz—again supposing the man and his diary had been legitimate, Ramsay reminded himself—had claimed that only a few Donnersprache devices had ever existed. And that Rudolf Hess, realizing the tremendous damage his idol Hitler had done through Donnersprache, had stolen one of the sealed units and defected to the British in May, 1941.

One of Parker's notes cited a quote from the famed Shirer text in which Hitler, discovering the flight of his most trusted accomplice, shouted, "I've got to talk to Goering right away!" *No wonder,* Ramsay mused, *if Goering and Hess had been the curators of the Donnersprache machines.*

But Hess, in a stolen Messerschmitt 110, had not landed as he'd intended in Scotland. Bedeviled by weather and without a landing field for the skittish Messerschmitt, Hess had parachuted to safety while the aircraft crashed. This much was history. According to the Mainz account, Hess had either been unable to bail out with the Donnersprache unit, or else it had been wrenched from his grasp when the chute opened. In either case, when the device hit the ground its case ruptured, and after the ensuing explosion nothing could have been left but scattered, anonymous debris. By the time Hess was interrogated the man was an emotionally shattered wreck, lapsing into madness, speaking of strange forces by which men could be moved.

Richard Parker's suspicions were that, during the brief alliance with Stalin, Hitler or one of his staff had told the Soviets something about Donnersprache. Hess himself had loathed everything Russian and had gone from internment with the Brits straight to Nuremberg for his trial, then to Spandau Prison where American, British, French, and

Russian jailers had watched Hess when they were not watching each other.

"That'll play," Ramsay mused aloud. "The Sovs couldn't get anything out of Hess so they made damned sure he'd never leave Spandau. Yeah. Yeah?" He barked a short laugh at himself and let the page drop onto the surface of his kitchen passthrough, as if by this gesture he could just as easily drop the whole matter. Ignore it as the ravings of a lunatic; several lunatics, in fact, all with the same paranoid fantasy.

He microwaved a passable Fettucine Alfredo and made himself a salad, dicing the tomato into cubes so small that Kathleen had called them lumpy catsup, snipping green onions over the romaine because he wouldn't be breathing on anyone this night, thinning the Roquefort dressing with yogurt to limit its calories. He chose a Lowenbrau from the refrigerator. From time to time he caught himself glancing toward the passthrough, keeping a wary eye on that single page as though it might burst into flame at any moment.

He ate at the little kitchen table, too preoccupied to select a recording of what he called wallpaper music, the sort of music made famous by Tangerine Dream which Kathleen had scorned but which helped Ramsay unwind. Time was when he would have talked this out with Kathleen (never Kathy, never Kate, never *ever* Katie, always insisting that a reporter named Katie or Kathy would never get the respect of a Kathleen, and asking who would ever have unburdened himself to a Babs Walters) because Kathleen was a better investigative reporter than she ever was a wife. Well, he still could debate it with her, as easily as picking up the phone; but he wouldn't. Their only bond now was Laurie, if you discounted occasional letches between ex-spouses who feared AIDS more than they craved variety.

No, not Kathleen. Who might he bounce this against at NBN? Britt? Ynga? No, this was too unlikely, yet so goddamn *big* if it had any legitimacy at all! He'd just have to research it himself, source it to hell and gone, as the spooks liked to say, or simply brand it as a curious hallucination and forget about it, a feat of which Ramsay was simply incapable; and Ramsay knew it.

He reached out for the memocomp notepad at the kitchen phone and began to list items that might be verifiable. If, and only if, everything tallied he might start checking on the likelihood that a human voice could be massaged and enhanced enough to make it, effectively, the voice of charismatic appeal. A George Whitefield voice; a Bryan voice. Perhaps even a Judy Garland voice, begging only for love.

Or an Adolf Hitler voice, commanding hate.

Dieter Mainz, Innsbruck; daughter? he wrote.

German electronics advances 1930, he added.

And *Goering—Reichstag tunnel,* and *Hess flight,* and *Shirer quote,* and finally *Kalvin bio.* This last item would be in NBN files and was as simple a matter as patching the modem in his study into NBN's computer.

But if, by some tremendous long shot, this tale had any substance, then the government's own electronic ears might be alert for anyone who became curious about Walter Kalvin. It was known that the National Security Agency's electronic monitors could flag a key word from a hundred thousand simultaneous telephone calls, maybe more. It followed that the monitors might also flag a request by a private modem. How much power could a White House administrator assemble in six months; enough to set requirements for NSA and CIA? Not unless he had the obedient help of the President of the United States.

Ramsay had attended many a White House news conference, and had seen the new President off the record, in unguarded moments. It was Ramsay's feeling that Harrison Rand's mental wattage would not run a nightlight,

though he was certainly a likeable cuss. As likeable as
Harding, or Reagan. A vagrant tagline tugged at his mind:
The paranoids are out to get me. . . .

"Christ, it's catching," he muttered aloud, and reached
for the phone.

He did not call NBN, but punched the number on Matthew Alden's elegant buff stationery. He reached a message recorder and had just given his name, halfway through
a recitation of his own unpublished number, when he was
interrupted by a brisk New England baritone. "Mr. Ramsay? Matt Alden here. I recognize your voice." Alden did
not bother to apologize. Ramsay often did the same thing,
listening to a caller before choosing to go on-line. One of
the prices of celebrity. . . .

"I just got your envelope, Mr. Alden. If you prefer, I
could call another—"

Alden: "No, no, perfectly all right." Then the silence
of a man who knew how to wait.

"I think we should speak in generalities, Mr. Alden."

"Matt, please. Just a moment; there. I'm no longer recording and we can consider this a privileged conversation, Mr. Ramsay."

"Alan will do. What I need is some way to contact your
friend, the one who doesn't strain at trifles. Do you have
any idea, any at all, what his letter was about specifically?"

"Specifically? Not the foggiest, but I presumed it had
something to do with one of your—"

"Okay, good. I'm serious about generalities, Matt."

"Uh—understood. My acquaintance did imply that if I
chose to answer any questions—and I suppose that would
apply to you as well—I could regret it."

Ramsay, with a chuckle: "If I were amateur enough to
tell more than I asked, yes. Not a problem, Matt."

"I suppose not. And I don't want to wander into a can
of worms."

"Not if I can help it. But I'd like to contact your acquaintance directly. It would take you out of the loop,"
Ramsay added the inducement.

Alden: "Uh-huh. I can give you something along that
line, if he concurs. Actually, he'd be more likely to contact
you than the other way around. It's just as well because,
frankly, I'm beginning to want out of this loop. Ah—if
acting as an innocent conduit somehow puts me at risk,
you *will* be good enough to warn me?"

"The chances are one in a million, but it's the least I
can do," Ramsay replied.

Alden: "I didn't quite hear you say yes."

Ramsay, laughing: "Yes, and yes again. My sources are
privileged too; I never made this call. Anything more?"

Alden: "Just keep up the good work. Good to meet
you, Alan."

Ramsay: "And you, Matt. Good night."

Ten minutes later, Ramsay realized he was still standing
by the phone, and by then it was too late to call Laurie.
It wasn't too late to do some research from an anonymous
computer terminal in the National Press Building, though.
These days the historic old structure at Fourteenth and F
was open around the clock. Like as not, a gaggle of domestic and foreign press people would be arguing, working, and boozing until the early hours.

He cursed the lock and the balky door of the garage he
rented a block from his apartment, promising himself for
the hundredth time that he'd install an automatic opener,
knowing he never would. The shovel-nosed little Genie
coupe, his one adult toy, squatted inside with the gleam
of a yellow opal in a tarnished setting. Five minutes later
it was fully warmed, squirting southwest on U.S. 1 while
Ramsay inhaled cool night air. Soon he could smell the
reek of the Potomac tidal basin, and minutes later he found
press parking.

His ID was enough union card to get him past all the
reconditioned bricabrac to the National Press Club's lair
on the building's top floor. Few of his colleagues in electronic media spent much time here, but a reporter could
call up any number of data services at any hour—including
the Library of Congress—on an unused terminal without
using his personal ID. He spied a terminal carrel in a
corner, exchanged nods with a pair of newsmen who
scarcely interrupted their discussion in fluent French, fed
coins into an espresso machine, then took the bitter,
steaming brew to the carrel and unfolded the small rectan-
gle on which he had made his list.

The Shirer citation was the simplest to verify. Using a
fast-search program through the full text, three-quarters of
a million words, Ramsay soon verified a quotation and,
moments later on page 192, learned that Nazi thugs had
traversed a tunnel from Goering's residence to torch the
mighty Reichstag. Nor was Shirer the only source to describe this event as Nazi arson. *A pretty drastic way to
remove evidence of wiretaps in a building*, Ramsay
thought. *But Goering was known for his drastic measures.*
The motive offered for the fire was a manufactured provocation to round up German leftists. Ramsay reminded
himself that an act may have more than one motive, and
kept checking.

Three sources described Rudolf Hess's uniform dis-
guise—as a captain—when stealing the Messerschmitt he
piloted to Scotland. Only one mentioned the fact that he
carried a smallish piece of luggage, ostensibly in case of
an emergency landing. Ramsay thought about that for a
long time before he shut down the terminal, wiped the
keyboard down with a tissue, and strolled to another terminal some distance away.

The state of the electronics art in Germany in 1930 was
not as easily learned by computer terminal. Parent com-
panies seemed to have sprung like weeds from the poly-

technic institute at Karlsruhe after the pioneering electronic work of Hertz; Badenwerke and Telefunken had grown from such work, cross-pollinated by Marconi, force-fed by military research in World War One. By 1928, Germany had fallen behind in commercial applications, but her research in electronics was paving the way for the independent development of radar. And in the psychological responses to audio stimuli, the few research papers before 1930 were virtually all German. No German citations in the field after 1931; no replications, no refinements; almost as if the German interest had abruptly died. *Or as if it had been curtained off,* Ramsay thought.

He wiped this terminal down, too, and decided against calling up the biography of cool, self-confident Walter Kalvin. NBN would have such stuff printed out in a file anyway, where Ramsay could read it anonymously. Now that Cody Martin's letter was starting to look like the story of the century, every step in researching it would have to be made on tiptoe.

If anyone had tried to share the elevator, Ramsay would have refused to enter it. He stepped outside, only two blocks from the White House, into a chill midnight wind bearing too much rain. It was no match for the blizzard howling through the mind of Alan Ramsay.

FOUR

Though the hour was late in the cloistered room adjoining his Oval Office, the President remained fresh and clear-eyed. Cabinet and council members often remarked on the stamina of Harrison Rand, unaware that their President's afternoon 'study hour' was really a ninety minute nap. Harry Rand had once joked to good old Walt Kalvin, his closest friend, that from two-thirty to four every day, Walt himself was President. Kalvin had not seemed to enjoy the joke, perhaps because others were present.

Harry sometimes regretted this lack of risibility on the part of his friend; had even prayed to the Lord to give Walter Kalvin a sense of humor, though it was plain He had more important things to do because, while Walt knew how to laugh in public, he retained the cold intensity of dry ice and all the good humor of a headstone. People said that Harry Rand, in private, was exactly the same as President Harrison Rand in public, and this pleased him because, as he used to tell his Missouri congregation, what you see ought to be what you get.

Some had forced comparisons between this Harry and another Harry from Missouri who had occupied the White House half a century before. It only bothered Harry Rand when they suggested that the other Harry had been a little swifter of thought, and more his own man.

Nobody had ever accused Harry Rand of special beauty, with his ruddy, round and open face, free-swinging expansive gestures, somewhat larger than life, given to bright vests that kept his belly in. He envied Walt Kalvin for his waist measurement, which had not changed on that wiry frame in the years since the two had met in Kansas City.

And Kalvin's friendship had led here, to the Oval Office—and, at the moment, to the small adjoining conference room in the West Wing. Lyndon Johnson had called it the little office; more recently it had been called the think tank. Beatrice Rand, in one of her first acts as First Lady, had refurbished it in euromodern style and now, alone with his chief advisor and half reclining in a pillowy lounge chair, Harry Rand rested the heels of his loafers on the top of a coffee table that floated on permanent magnets above its base.

Snazzy, weird and wildly expensive, Harry mused. *Lord, where would I be today without old Walt? Delivering benedictions back in KayCee, most likely.* He gazed with affection across the table at Kalvin, who was talking as he always was; explaining this, urging that. Often, Harry listened, sometimes with rapt attention when Walt called from the Executive Office Building just across the drive. You had to hand it to Walt, on a telephone or radiophone call the man was a demon of persuasiveness. But at other times—now, for example—Harry's mind tended to wander.

Why the heck didn't Walt accept an office in the West Wing, where we could talk face to face anytime his Pres-

ident wanted him? Well, Walt had a fetish about that; he had always, from the early days of that first bewildering senatorial race in Missouri, depended more on a good intercom system than face-to-face discussion. In fact, most of Walt Kalvin's special ideas seemed to develop best over the intercom. Which one of them was he pushing now? Harry Rand tuned his mind back to the man who sat facing him in a Barcelona chair, and caught Walt's drift after a moment. The Federal Media Council . . .

". . . Must have a more responsible press," Kalvin was saying, "if we want strong grass-roots support for your programs. There's nothing like bushels of mail from the public to move those hidebound bastards on Capitol Hill."

"Now, Walt," said Harry, with the sad little smile he always used when Kalvin became profane. "There's plenty of time to work that out."

"No, there isn't." Other presidential advisors were far more circumspect, would at least precede a flat disagreement by 'with all due respect, Mr. President,' but not old Walt when it was just the two of them. "Those codgers on the Hill are experts at wasting time. We've been in office five months now and they haven't brought the media council to a vote. Do you want an end to abortion and pornography and ecology freaks hamstringing good old American industry, or don't you?"

"But they won't be voting on those," Harry said.

Kalvin took a long breath, looked away, took a sip of his watered bourbon. Then, slowly and carefully, he said, "Harry, you won't get those programs enacted as long as the media is free to say absolutely anything that comes into its head, including things that amount to sedition. What have I been saying for the last twenty minutes?"

For the last twenty minutes, Harry Rand had been thinking about many things: which negligee Bea was wearing tonight, which talk show might have the most interesting guests, whether he should have liposuction in the fall—things like that. Surely a man who was devoting twelve hours a day to promoting a more decent God-fearing America ought to be allowed to let his brain rest before bedtime.

But no-o-o. Still, there was absolutely no question that his career depended on listening to Walter Kalvin. Walt even saw to such final details as microphone checks for press conferences, which irked Evan Showers, the Presidential Press Secretary, no end. And every time, *every blessed time,* Harry publicly proposed some program that Walt had warned him against, the response was lackluster at best. At worst, it was hostile. Lord, Lord, how your flock can jostle you at times! "You've been saying you want to control the media," Harry sighed.

Kalvin's hand went up quickly, like that of a cop directing traffic. "No, no; one word you never use about media is 'control,' Harry. I mean, everybody loves you, that's what I realized fifteen years ago, that's how we got here; but by everybody, I don't mean *every*body. Think how a Jew reacts to a swastika, and you'll get some idea how a newspaper editor or a TV commentator reacts to the idea of control. And unless I'm very much mistaken, the kind of person who tends not to love you is a cynic, and that's exactly the sort of person the media is full of."

"Don't you mean, 'are full of'? Media is plural, isn't it?"

Another long pause. "*Are* full of, Harry. I don't care, Harry. Harry, can we just . . . just focus on the problem here? The only grammar rule I'm interested in right now is that you never use the word 'control' in a sentence dealing with media. What you talk about instead is *responsibility.* We've had responsible media during wartime, more or less. And we've had temporary commissions, federal bodies with the teeth to chew ass, during those times.

"What you want, Harry, is teeth that aren't temporary.

We don't call it a task force or a commission, that sounds too much like, ah—''

"Mustn't say it," said the President, smiling, reaching for his own highball.

"Right. You call it a council. The image of a deliberative body, one that mulls things over and recommends things. Only this one can levy a fine—pick a number—or jerk a broadcasting license. That, Harry, is how you get a bunch of uncontr—unGodly media liberals to go easy on the criticism."

Harry Rand took a sip. "Then we sweep pornography from the shelves," he said.

"Yes."

A larger sip. "Then we cast out the coat hangers."

"Wha—ah, the abortionist's coat hanger; sometimes you come up with unexpected connections, Harry. But yes; out with the coat hangers."

Harry drained his glass. "It sounds good, Walt, I'll get back to you on it."

"Or I can call you."

"I was sure you would," said the President. "But I don't see why the urgency."

Kalvin swirled his drink and took his time answering. "It gets a little complicated. Call it a window of opportunity. I thought it would stay open, but it won't."

"Don't go cryptic on me," said the President.

"All right: I know how you worry about people and I didn't want to bother you. And he would be very upset if he knew I'd told you, so this doesn't go out of the room."

Harry drew a cross-my-heart on his vest. "Who'd be upset?"

"Terence Unruh. He has an inoperable cancer, Harry. He'll be dead in six weeks."

Harry Rand frowned his way to a connection. "Oh; that CIA deputy you're so chummy with. Family man?"

"Yes, but they're taking it well. And the Director of

Central Intelligence will pick the next man. And whoever he is, he won't be as, um, friendly as Terry Unruh. We have a month, Harry. After that, if we've lost our unofficial friendly provider and we can't make sure the media are responsible to us, I couldn't guarantee anything."

Harry Rand knew that Walt's definition of 'friendly' leaned toward the willing and useful; the manageable of whatever Walter Kalvin wanted managed. "Don't look so glum, Walt." Pointing at his breast, smiling: "This is still where all the bucks stop."

Walter Kalvin's glance was almost dismissive. "I wouldn't guarantee even that, Harry," he said. "You never know what ridiculous charges might get ballyhooed into an issue by some gonzo newsman. But with a Federal Media Council, you can stop the ballyhoo before it gains momentum."

Harry Rand could feel himself flushing with irritation because, while he bowed to no man in his basic goodness, this council idea was the sort of thing that might work for men whose supply of goodness was severely limited. He stood up, walked to the ritzy rosewood panel and waved a hand where the capacitance switch would sense it, so that the panel slid aside to reveal the ice and the bourbon. "I've always wondered if cancer was God's justice. Is Terence Unruh an evil man, Walt?"

Speaking to the President's back, Kalvin said, "He's one of your most ardent supporters. But no man's closet is entirely without its skeletons. You wouldn't deny that, you of all people."

Harry Rand wheeled, ignoring the slosh of Wild Turkey on his fingers. "No, but I can sincerely regret it. God has forgiven my youthful sins, Walter. Why can't you?"

The use of the full name, 'Walter,' was not lost on Kalvin. Harry did not use it often. "I forgave you. Bea wouldn't, but I did. I've even pulled a few strings to help the, um, vessel of your sin in her career. You didn't know that, did you?''

Harry started on the fresh drink, no longer feeling so fresh himself. "No. But now that I do, I bet you could reach her any time you wanted to.''

A shrug. "She's somewhere around, I think.''

"In Washington?" With the sensation of ants chewing their way up the back of his neck, Harry was definitely feeling wilted.

"I think so," Kalvin said as though it were of no importance. "Can't expect a pretty Albuquerque girl to stay there forever. Besides, this is where the jobs are. And she thinks too highly of you to ever be a problem, Harry.''

Harry Rand made a silent prayer, not for absolution but for deliverance. The girl had been his only stray step from the straight and narrow, but try telling that to Bea! And somewhere around the District of Columbia tonight, that pretty little time bomb was ticking away. . . . "Who does she work for?''

Walt Kalvin rarely smiled, and when he did, it made him look sly. He was looking sly now. "Interested in her again?''

"No! Not the way you mean. I could always ask someone else," said the President, knowing full well his old friend Walt would rather be his only channel of information.

"She works for a man named Tate.''

"Who's he?''

Standing up, speaking quickly now: "Who does consulting for us through Showers, but Tate's made it plain she should listen to a man named Lathrop, who works for Terry Unruh at Langley.''

"You're telling me that sweet little creature is a CIA employee," said the President.

"She doesn't know it but indirectly, yes. She does know that she works for you.''

"Loyal little thing," murmured Harry Rand, thinking, *If I'd been single and twenty years younger* . . . . "Well, I'm glad you saw to her welfare, Walt, though I wonder what you were thinking of, getting her a job in this town. And I repeat, I don't want to face that temptation again, so you just see to it that I don't." He knew that Kalvin was sensitive enough to his moods that, when his soul was uneasy, even Walter Kalvin trod with care. "I'm going to bed now."

Kalvin stood up, drained his glass. "Just keep in mind that we'd better have a media council before Unruh starts sipping morphine cocktails. When we can nail a reporter for sedition, we won't need a replacement for Unruh. If we can't—because Unruh could be your Ollie North to an irresponsible press—consider packing your bags a couple of months from now."

Tugging at his vest, preparing for the walk from the West Wing back to the White House proper, the President paused at the door. "I suppose you've given some thought to the people I might appoint to that council."

"Some," Walt Kalvin agreed. "And to chair it, why, as it happens I have a little spare time I might devote to it. Any problem with that?"

"No," said the President moodily. "I was just hoping you might surprise me."

FIVE

RAMSAY AWOKE WITH A POSSIBLE SOLUTION FOREMOST IN his mind, the perch his sleep had clung to, a springboard for a Friday morning scrubbed clean by the rain; and its name was T. Broeck Wintoon. Ramsay made it out Connecticut Avenue to the studios before nine, not driving hard but with a sense of urgency. One day NBN would abandon this sprawl of offices across the second story of a suburban shopping center; go for status like ABC. And then Alan Ramsay would really have something to bitch about: parking, congestion, formality.

No need for a guard at the back entrance because his keycard was his pass through the steel-faced door, and Ramsay took the stairs three at a time. A cheery greeting to Ellen at the reception desk, a quick scan of the big board in the middle of the 'bullpen,' a room larger and noisier than it should be for professionals sweating deadlines. He was in time for the early conference session for the evening news—here in the studios they called it the nice capades because several tough prima donnas managed to put broadcasts together every day by simply nicing like hell, being objective about the length and placement of their stories. That, like working in an atmosphere of simulated chaos, was also part of professionalism.

His next piece wasn't scheduled until Monday. He even had time for the call to old Wintoon, so Ramsay swung into his glassed-in cubicle and punched the information number for Georgetown University. Professor Wintoon, with only two classes to meet and a penchant for popping in on fellow academics, was seldom in his office. That's why the old man carried a pager on his belt, calling Ramsay back from the faculty lounge.

"Thought we could have lunch," Ramsay found himself saying after mutual greetings. Jesus, he couldn't just blurt this kind of thing out without preamble! "I'm researching a piece on the laserboost cargo system"—that much was true enough—"and wanted to tap your head on the international relations angle."

Wintoon had done a CIA tour back in the sixties. An old family friend, Broeck Wintoon had developed wisdom with his caution and he had more solid gold contacts than Bell Labs. The familiar gravel-dry voice was vibrant as ever. "The view of an unimpeachable, low-tech source, Alan? I'm no engineer."

Ramsay agreed, chuckling, that he needed something from a generalist with credibility, and mentioned their last talk six months previous without referring to its substance. Wintoon would realize instantly that the intelligence community was again, somehow, part of the topic. Wintoon was booked for lunch, sorry, but would be in the Med School library after that. "Until cocktail time," the old fellow added. "If you'd care to join me at my club?"

"Booze breath is a no-no when I'm on deadline," Ramsay said lightly, though his own deadline was very personal, promising to drop by the campus in midafternoon.

He put the phone down feeling better, then hurried to collect his materials for the nice capades. Irv, the producer, would forgive anything but lack of preparation.

Ramsay's upcoming piece would deal with the fleet of laserboosted pilotless cargo vessels now in development in central California. Dubbed 'Highjump,' the system featured a fleet of small orbital vehicles that would soon be delivering half-ton cargoes to America's half-assembled space station on an hourly basis. A National Public Radio feature had already hinted that, while Highjump's laserboost was nonpolluting and many times cheaper than chemical propulsion, it could also become the basis for an orbital bombardment scheme.

Ramsay thought Highjump no more warlike than the Sov and Japanese spaceplanes, yet he was far from any conclusions. That's what research and videotaped interviews were for.

He fidgeted throughout the session with Irv, unable to concentrate, remembering the letter in his jacket pocket. He carried the session off, though, with promises and memocomp notes. One of those notes, on a line by itself, was simply BIO. As if he could forget.

Despite the handy terminals, Ramsay went straight to the station's wall-length array of file cabinets. NBN had found that some people simply worked better from paper than from a screen, and let the obsolete file system remain. There, he found several updates to the bio on Kalvin, Walter Franz, beginning with the Missouri primary back during the eighties.

Instead of letting an aide do the photocopy work, Ramsay made inferior copies in Irv's spare office using his pocket copier. The problem with pocket copiers was that they either made reduced copies that only a kid could read without squinting, or they required that your pocket be the size of an attaché case. Ramsay chose to squint rather than carry a purse. He took the copies with him to lunch,

gnawing an order of barbecued ribs while parked in the
Zoological Gardens with the Genie's top retracted.

He knew most of the Kalvin bio already from the Martin
letter, though he was both excited and frightened to find
Martin's details confirmed. Foreign-born but naturalized,
degree from NYU. Enlisted in the Air Force, served in
Germany, fluent in German. Later a master's from Cornell
in electronic engineering, a totally different discipline from
his NYU bachelor's, but military training sometimes
broadened a young man's horizons and educated him in
the process. Postgrad work at Stanford, experimental psychology and psychoacoustics, but no doctorate. Several
years in Southern California in the recording industry.
Then a staff member in the political machine that had
elected a dark horse latino as mayor of Los Angeles. The
mayor had later been recalled.

Kalvin seemed to have had no work for the next two
years but surfaced next in Kansas City—in the retinue of
a crusading preacher who ran, successfully, for the Senate,
then captured the Republican nomination and the White
House itself. Walter Franz Kalvin, White House Chief of
Staff, was now enjoying the perks of an indispensable man.
Pundits had joked for nearly two centuries about the informal Presidential advisory groups that functioned parallel with official cabinets, but in Kalvin's case some wag
had dubbed him Rand's entire pantry.

Ramsay rechecked his notes; yes, Kalvin had switched
from Demo to GOP—but so what? He'd also switched from
rhetoric to Air Force intelligence to electronics to experimental psychology to recording studios, and finally to politics. It seemed to make no sensible pattern. Unless you
plugged in the wildest tale imaginable, a man who somehow recovered an electronic device a half-century old with
the potential to persuade people—a hell of a lot of people.

A man with a master's in electronics could have minia-
turized a breadbox-sized rig of the thirties, especially with

the facilities of a recording studio at his disposal. He could also have tried his stuff out with the speeches of a mayoral candidate; evidently with success. *And after that, what? Took your time, didn't you, looking for a likeable cuss who had the right background, the right voice, and a willingness to be led.*

Ramsay drove back to the studios with more care than usual, viewing himself objectively as a man who must not come to harm before passing on what he had. Then he managed somehow to channel his mind toward the Highjump piece, taking one telephoned interview and making two appointments.

But midafternoon found him nosing the yellow Genie off Reservoir Road toward the Med School library. As promised, Wintoon was waiting. The very image of an erect, tweedy old lecturer, Broeck Wintoon kept his white hair cut short, almost military, and Ramsay envied his tan. Wintoon's long legs easily outpaced Ramsay up a long stair to an enclosed carrel, both men chatting about family ties as they went. Once inside the air-conditioned room they moved on to a brief interchange about uses to which the Pentagon might put the Highjump program, and the reactions of other nations to the system. Ramsay unlimbered his little videotaper, got Wintoon to expand on a few points before a wide-angle lens, the Georgetown U. hospital building a sturdy background prop through the carrel window.

"The most common response is a waiting line among small nations to piggyback their own experiments on Highjump vehicles," Wintoon finished, "except for Canada. She's building the orbital dock facility for the system, so the Canadians are, shall we say, high on the concept." The gray eyes twinkled with his double entendre, and Ramsay grinned as he reviewed what he had by fast monitor through the auxiliary eyepiece.

"Perfect," Ramsay murmured, and slipped the recorder into a pocket. "So much for reality. There's something else, though. Maybe I should've worn a straitjacket."

"Might cause talk," Wintoon smiled, studying the younger man with the patient alertness of an old falcon. He stood up and flexed his arms, then folded them, still looking into Ramsay's eyes. "Old business, or new business?" he prompted. The lines around his pale eyes crinkled in lively curiosity.

"New to me, and goddamned disturbing," Ramsay admitted, and took a deep breath. "Is there any question of, um, domestic political intrigue so potent that you wouldn't want to hear it?"

Wintoon's smile grew cool and distant. He hadn't thought in such terms for years, he replied, but he guessed not. Ramsay asked if the name Cody Martin rang any bells; Wintoon said no, but he knew hardly anyone at field agent level these days. Was Martin one of the retired spooks he'd met at some high-level seminar?

"I gather it's a beard anyway," Ramsay said, without mentioning the Alden connection, and reached inside his jacket. "The guy sent this to me in care of the Overseas Press Club. It works," he shrugged.

"Good cutout for sensitive information," Wintoon nodded, accepting the folded paper, tugging a set of half-glasses from a pocket. He read without visible reaction for a few moments, then glanced over the tops of his glasses with an exaggerated lift of both eyebrows.

Ramsay knew that sign. One raised eyebrow equaled clear skepticism; both raised meant dangerous ground. He watched the old man sit down, attention riveted on what he read, scratching absently at loose folds of skin at his throat.

Wintoon read to the end, then swiveled in his chair and gazed across the building tops of Washington for some time. Then: "Kalvin," he muttered, and his smile was

accusing. "I watched your 'True Believer' commentary,
Alan. This is such a pat answer, all aside from the, ah . . ."

"Wacko element?"

"Well—a sendup, perhaps."

"Goering burned the Reichstag. Hess escaped Germany
with a piece of luggage that was never found or explained,
and the Sovs let him rot in Spandau. Walter Kalvin was in
Air Force Intelligence in Germany and speaks fluent German, did you know that?"

Wintoon shook his head, his gaze expectant.

"Kalvin is bright, nobody denies that; but how many
guys get a degree in rhetoric and then a second one in
electronics? Takes extra courses in psychoacoustics, then
spends a few years gimmicking bad music for teenybop-
pers in a recording studio?"

"Facts?"

"In his bio," Ramsay shrugged. "Then got a latino
elected mayor of L.A., maybe for practice, and finally
showed up joined to Harrison Rand like a Siamese twin
before Rand made his political bid in Missouri. Now this
accusation turns up in the secret files of a murdered Undersecretary of State. You see why I've got sweaty palms?"
Wintoon's face was now a study in impassivity, carefully
noncommittal. Ramsay took the letter back, folded it, and
continued, "This guy Martin wrote to me because of my
big mouth on NBN. I need a face-to-face with him, and
somebody to pass this on to while I'm still healthy. You'd
know whether I should hit on somebody—cabinet member, one of the Joint Chiefs—*who*?"

Wintoon had always given clear signals when reluctant
to pursue a topic. This time, he promised pursuit at his
own rarefied levels, and also promised a reply. The old
man ended by reassuring Ramsay: however high the pile
of evidence, it was all circumstantial. A real connection
between the murder of Richard Parker and the clout of

Walter Kalvin was a million-to-one shot. Not to worry, Alan.

Ramsay hurried downstairs with Wintoon, agreeing as they parted that they must keep in closer touch, assuring Wintoon that little Laurie was indeed becoming a young lady. Alan Ramsay would have embraced his mentor had he suspected that this might be the last time he would ever clasp the hand of the old warrior-savant.

After feeding the Wintoon interview tape into his active files at the studios, Ramsay sought more high-tech expertise on Highjump. His third call turned up a civilian analyst at the nearby Naval Observatory who was willing to give him an interview. The best time would be tomorrow, Saturday afternoon, when the major activity on the site was a basic youth tour—a new public relations gambit stressing the excitement of space development. Ramsay agreed; rang off wondering how he would shoehorn the interview into his weekend with Laurie, and suddenly realized his windfall. Moments later, he had Kathleen on the telephone.

"Nothing to do with military stuff," he objected to Kathleen's objection. "Basic astronomy, science, orbital industry. We both know Laurie's a little pacifist, thanks to you. Why not let her decide whether she wants to go?"

There were blonde voices and brunette voices, he thought, and for a blonde, Kathleen had a very dark voice when provoked. "Why not help her decide, you mean."

"For a parent, it's no felony. You know how I feel, Kathleen."

"You bet I do, you feel with both hands. Not too bad for an old lecher, if memory serves." Here it came; at the damnedest times, but not unwelcome.

"Uh, you could get served, maybe serviced is more like it, tonight, and I could stay over and take Laurie tomor—"

"Busy tonight," she said quickly. Kathleen always resorted to quick telegraphic phrases when hoping to pass over something. A date, no doubt, with some schmuck she wouldn't let into bed. But she'd dazzle him, get herself primed, and then use Ramsay to pump her empty a day later.

Well, it could be worse; the other way around, for example. "So when can I be of service, madame?"

She took the cue, saying she would play the madame on Saturday night, and he jollied her into putting Laurie on the phone extension, feeling as if he'd peddled his cock for the privilege. Then Laurie came on-line, faintly surly as usual when he hadn't called for a day or so. *All right, three days. Is that a crime?* He knew that in Laurie's statutes, it was. "Hi, pudd'n. How would you like a live multimedia show after lunch tomorrow?"

"If you have time," she said, making him come to her.

He did: "Pudd'n, I couldn't call earlier," he slurred, courting the damn kid with kid talk, powerless with his own daughter. Then he invented a reason for not calling, a story so patently and transparently false that Laurie was soon giggling, helping him invent it. By then, he knew that Laurie would be stumping her plump eleven-year-old buns off at the U.S. Naval Observatory the next day, while he ducked out for half an hour to tape an interview.

And by then, as weekend traffic began to clog highway arterials in the nation's capital, Professor T. Broeck Wintoon had begun to inquire about the Martin letter; very cautious, wise inquiries near the very top of the old-boy network, although he knew that caution and wisdom are pale qualities in the beam of raw power.

Kalvin, who seldom put in less than a twelve-hour day between the White House and this office he had requisitioned on the third floor of the Executive Office Building, was not surprised when his own secretary's chime sounded on his desk intercom at seven P.M. Millicent knew better than to leave before he did. The surprise was that this particular caller was standing in her office.

"Certainly, let him in, Millie. Oh, I'll lock up tonight. I'll bet you've got some man waiting. You be on time Monday," he added.

"Thank you, sir," was the dulcet response. Millie might be as unlovely as snow tries, but she had a voice cultured by generations of Virginians and she knew when she was being told to get lost. The door snicked and Kalvin stood up as his caller walked in.

The first thing Kalvin said was, "Was this wise? You could have called by scrambler."

"Not for this," Unruh said, sitting down unbidden as though made of some brittle substance. "Terminal action always takes a face-to-face, Walt."

"Have a drink? You're looking good," Kalvin remarked, turning toward his ornate bar cabinet.

"I look like the wrath of God and you know it," said the CIA deputy. "This fucking hairpiece doesn't fit, and I wonder why I let them do the chemotherapy anyhow. Nothing for me, thanks," he waved the notion aside as Kalvin raised a bottle aloft.

"What's this about terminal action?" Kalvin asked, dropping ice into his scotch, sitting down with robotic precision. Privately he admitted that Terry Unruh looked like bloody hell, his blonde hairpiece failing to match the remaining wisps of gray at his ears, the lank frame more cadaverous each time he saw the man. But Unruh knew how to keep a bargain, staying on the job as long as he could stand up, satisfied with the weekly deposits to the Bermuda bank because they would serve as a magnificent widow's pension.

"One of my colleagues sent a rocket up my arse not a half-hour ago. There's an ex-Company man, an academic near retirement, zeroing in on Parker and connecting us with him. I don't know the old boy's source."

His posture frozen, Kalvin said it as a simple fact: "We have to find out. Fast."

"Apparently the old fellow hinted that major media is asking. He knows everybody in this town so it could be anybody."

"Shit. Just when we think we've put a lid on it," Kalvin said into his glass. "Okay: you must have a cure, or you wouldn't be here."

"You could call it a cure: surgery. I have the scalpel en route from Quebec. Foreign, plausibly deniable, and a very, very subtle interrogator. Doesn't leave marks." Unruh cocked his head, regarding Kalvin without pleasure: "Did you know that the most terrifying thing a man can feel is slow asphyxiation? Utter panic sets in, you have to see it to—"

"That's enough," said Kalvin. "You do what you have to, and so do I."

"I wonder about that," Unruh murmured.

"Wonder and be damned," said Kalvin, "so long as you provide for your family, and that means providing a few things for me." He took a long appreciative sip. "Do I know your, ah, expendable academic?"

A shrug. "Name's Wintoon; moderately strong profile in some circles. But we may be looking at some *really* high profiles, maybe in media."

"For that you have to bring in an outsider?"

"Some things the Company can do. Some, it subcontracts to certain provider groups. A few things, the Company just doesn't condone, and my assets on this are three people, four if you count this Canadian mercenary, because you wanted to keep it small and manageable. The Quebec scalpel does things nobody wants to know about, but you can bet two things. He'll be sanitary, and he won't terminate the interview until he gets all there is to get,"

Unruh said in tones that were dead flat. "I can call it off, of course. I'm here to get your orders."

Kalvin studied the features of the dying Unruh through the flat facets of his glass. The pale face remained mask-like, but Walter Kalvin felt a sudden intuition about what was going on behind that mask as Unruh, with the effort of an exhausted man, stood up. Terence Unruh would probably much rather terminate Kalvin himself than have it done to some doddering old onetime spook. "Then do what's necessary, Terry. Just make absolutely certain you get to the root of this. We can't start laying waste to everybody in Washington. And get back to me as soon as you have the results of the, um, operation. By scrambler. I'll be here."

Unruh nodded; turned toward the door.

"Oh, and Terry?" The man stopped at Kalvin's words, twisting at the waist as if too tired to take extra steps. "Don't come here again. You do look like the wrath of God, that's a fact. You take away a man's appetite."

"Thank you very much, your excellency," said Unruh as he moved through the doorway.

Alone, Kalvin tapped his teeth against the edge of his glass and checked his watch. He'd have time for a good dinner, something light with a sparkling wine, maybe pick up a historical novel from the Waldenbooks place on the mall, and then return to the office. He felt certain that even Unruh's deniable scalpel would not be operating at full speed before dark.

SIX

LATE IN THE EVENING, RAMSAY HAULED A SNACK FROM the kitchen microwave unit and took it back to his half-read book in Laurie's room, which doubled as his study since the divorce. He'd had the choice of a ballet, a party, or an evening with the book. A good party outranked most books, but not the three G's, Goddard, Goldman and Greenleaf; and a leg man with Ramsay's eye would only have been frustrated by ballerinas. He picked up the Goddard paperback and succumbed to its sinister influence, and cursed himself for jumping when the phone jangled at his elbow.

"Yes," he said, giving nothing away. Then: "Did the station give you this number?—I did?—Oh, right, I did," he agreed, suddenly beaming. Damned right he had, not expecting her to call. That party at Ynga Lindermann's over a month before; he'd seen Pamela Garza among public relations people a couple of times but never knew her name until that party. Well, now. . . . "No, Pam, I really meant it. Soccer's a favorite of mine, give me the Diplomats over the Redskins any day.''

Pam Garza sounded more sunny and less smoky than she looked, if his memory was accurate. ''I have passes to watch this Bolivian guy's tryouts with the Dips. Very hush-hush,'' she said, tentatively, almost shyly, with a soft southwest drawl.

''Don't miss it,'' he advised, and listened for a moment. ''Me? Uh, yeah, love to. And I'll spring for a bite to eat afterward, *quid pro quo*—so long as I don't have to wear a tie.'' *Why the hell do I always have to say dumb things like that?*

''It's a deal,'' she laughed. ''Tomorrow afternoon at three.''

''Wups. No, wait, we can make it if you don't mind a third party. My kid, Laurie; she spends alternate weekends with me.''

''There's always another woman,'' she said with a theatrical sigh. ''Actually, I'd be honored, Alan. We can meet at RFK Stadium, main entrance, they said. Marvelous,'' she added. He had been about to say that himself.

Ramsay thanked her and put the phone down near the fake poppies on the desk—Laurie's present, her 'forever flowers,' a false gaity to brighten the room she had vacated. ''Hell,'' he muttered, suddenly remembering that he'd promised Kathleen a therapeutic lay on Saturday night. But Pamela Garza was not likely to be in the picture after dinner, certainly not with Laurie in tow. Whatthehell. If this lovely southwest praline got *him* excited, Kathleen would be the beneficiary. Titty for tatty. He picked up the Goddard, smiling, and congratulated himself for staying home that night.

Saturday began well when he drove to Kathleen's place, she smirking sexily and mistaking his guilty look—he said nothing about gorgeous Garza—for restrained lust as they shared herb tea in her Georgetown condo. God *damn* but he hated herb tea! Ramsay wondered if there was any better tipoff to the belief that all nations truly wanted freedom, peace, and equality than a weakness for frigging herb tea. He was too canny to wonder out loud. Kathleen wore smart gray slacks and low heels, knowing he liked skirts and high heels, probably certain that he was a conquest regardless of what she wore.

Then Laurie whirlwinded down from her room with a single overnight bag, scissored her legs around his waist as he lifted her, smothered him with an innocent, frantic kiss-kiss, and all but dragged him out of the condo. Her blonde ponytail was the same, but the apple cheeks were losing some baby fat and she was growing relentlessly taller. In two years, he joked with Kathleen, the kid would need a steamer trunk for a weekend and would take her majesty's sweet time coming down a flight of stairs.

"You always liked a girl to take her time," said Kathleen, reaching slender arms overhead in a languid stretch that tightened the fabric over her breasts.

He laughed, advising her to hold that thought, while Laurie tugged him toward the Genie.

Saturday seemed to get better when, after shopping, he left Laurie with a harried tour guide at the Naval Observatory. Because the analyst, a dour Carolinian from Scotland Neck, gave a hell of an interview with hand-held models at his desk. A Highjump vehicle, he showed, was dedicated to a very special orbit to serve the space station. The laserboost needed accumulated energy and could not cycle the vehicles much faster than one every hour; a possible weapon against one target, but wholly impractical as a mass bombardment system. Ramsay put away his video recorder and went to find Laurie's tour group, feeling better about Highjump and world peace as well.

Laurie, ponytail swinging, bounced away with him to

the parking lot, chattering of her new-found interest. "Joo know, Dad, I could kick a ball a mile on the moon?"

"Did *you* know, pudd'n, that we barely have time for a slice of pizza before you watch the Diplomats try out a new forward from Bolivia who can probably kick a soccer ball clean around the moon?" She squealed with delight. Despite Kathleen's best efforts to make Laurie intolerant of any kind of violence, the girl played grade-school soccer with the total abandon of a mounted cossack.

As she wolfed pizza, Ramsay fed her the itinerary, carefully casual when he mentioned Pam Garza. Laurie could bridle at the idea of his keeping company with strange women. *Breeding will tell*, he thought. *She's a natural competitor, like her old man.*

He let Laurie toot the Genie's horn in the Mass Ave underpass and, near Union Station, noticed a dun Ford Probe behind him. Hadn't he seen one just like it in the parking lot of the pizza joint? A Probe lacked the visual pizazz and the nitrous oxide injection kick of his Genie, but with the right equipment it was one hell of a machine; maybe the best choice you could make when trailing a maneuverable Genie in traffic.

He waltzed the yellow Genie through the congestion onto Independence, grimly aware that the Probe was still visible in his rearview. He refused to change his plans, drove to the huge lot of RFK Stadium, and saw the Probe commit to the bridge leading to Capitol Heights. Someone had a map unfolded in the passenger seat; almost certainly tourists. *Or passing for tourists. Stop it, fool,* he chided himself. *They'll be chasing you with a butterfly net any day now.*

At first sight of Pamela Garza, Laurie slitted her eyes as if keying on a goalie. Black loafers, denim skirt, high-collar white cotton blouse of a silken sheen almost as sleek as Pam's long black hair which she wore in a loose bun. Her dark eyes shining under luxuriant brow arches, Pam

traded a smiling glance with Ramsay that suggested she
would take a child's jealousy with aplomb.

Once inside the echoing corridors of the stadium: "Hey,
I need to find the powder room," Pam announced, adding, "I could use company, Laurie."

Laurie went with her, still standoffish, but returned five
minutes later chatting with Pam as if they were old friends.
Ramsay caught Pam's wink as they filed into the lower
tiers of the stadium, and wondered if a shared *pissoir* made
sisters of them all. The woman knew her soccer, delight-
ing Laurie with tales of the sport back at the University
of New Mexico. As well as the day had begun, it seemed
to keep getting better; the Bolivian gave a heady demon-
stration of his skills on the field.

"We can sure use him," Pam enthused later as they
strolled toward the parking lot. "Laurie, did you see
how—what's wrong, Alan; forget something?"

Ramsay patted his pockets convincingly, with a slow
turn as if to retrace his steps. If that brown Ford had been
a rough tail, there might be a smooth one following them
out of the stadium, but no one followed them. He shrugged
off the feeling and said he'd found his keys after all, smiling down at his companions.

Pam, suddenly: "Laurie, do you get a crick in your
neck from looking up at your dad?"

"Sometimes. But I can jump up on him and you better
not," Laurie said artlessly.

"No fear," Pam said, her laugh unfeigned and throaty.
"But I can wear heels and *you* better not, missy. That's
my Honda," she pointed to a dusty red coupe. "I'll go
over and fix myself up. Why don't you two drive that yellow lightning bolt over and collect me?"

Walking hand-in-hand to the Genie, the two Ramsays
spoke of food, of Bolivians, and only once of Pam. "She
says her company has the government for a client. What's
a client?"

"Somebody who gives you a job, but you don't work for them all the time," Ramsay said. "Practically every company in Washington could say that, pudd'n."

"Like NBN?"

He chuckled and squeezed her hand. "Not yet, but they're trying," he said. "They're always trying." He did not expand on the idea, nor mention this Federal Media Council foolishness that most media were watching cautiously. Even if the council became law, he reflected, it probably would not exert any more power than the defunct Federal Communications Commission had.

Laurie brought him back to the present with, "She's pretty. But I like her," explaining volumes with the 'but.'

As Ramsay pulled up beside the red Honda, Pam stowed something, perhaps an extra compact, in her glove box and exited the car with a flash of turquoise. Now she wore spaghetti-strap heels and a kerchief side-tied at her throat, all of a blue to complement the skirt and Pam's natural latina color. Ramsay caught Laurie studying his face for reaction and hid his awe with, "It's never too early to think of food." It was much too early, he added silently, to be ogling Pam Garza as if she were dessert.

Then they argued, hilariously. Pam suggested La Nicoise.

Ramsay, flicking his open collar: "No tie, remember? And I deeply mistrust any meal served by a waiter on roller skates." He suggested Beowulf Pub.

"There's enough Beowulf in you already," Pam teased. "How about Old Budapest?"

Laurie: "Do they have cheeseburgers?"

Ramsay: "Probably, with an unpronounceable name and seven surly gypsy fiddlers. Isn't it halfway to Dulles?"

"Halfway to *Dallas*," Pam admitted, and pointed a finger at Laurie's nose. "You," she accused, "have probably never had a buffaloburger. Betcha. And you, sir, have never had a choice of two hundred beers."

"Not at one sitting," he hedged, "but there's always a first time." So they drove nearly to Georgetown and ate at the Brickskellar, a family saloon with a game room that kept Laurie squandering half-dollars long after dinner.

In that time he sketched some of his background for Pam, including his boyhood on a Nebraska farm and his entry into media as a sports announcer. He claimed the blame for his divorce, saying that Laurie made all his mistakes worthwhile.

He learned in turn that the Garzas had sharecropped near Tucumcari, and that Pam's revolt against tradition had included leaving the Catholic Church. "I'm not sure whether I'm a Methodist or a Baptist," she laughed. "I've tried both."

Working her way through school in Albuquerque, Pam said, she had then worked her way up the ladder of a local public relations firm and, offered a chance at similar work in the nation's capital, she had leaped at it. She also alluded to a youthful affair with an older man in Albuquerque an alliance that he soon broke off with the genuine mixed emotions of a family man. "I was dumb, of course," she added, "and he was dumber, but really a sweet man. I had no idea how important he'd—ah, well. No regrets, Alan." And adeptly, she changed the subject.

Then Laurie was standing at their booth. "Five more bucks," she promised, "and I can beat the golem."

"You *are* the golem," he said. "Isn't that a lot of shooting, kid? I thought it was against your principles."

"It's not real, Dad." She had always called him 'Daddy.' Was it possible that the girl was maturing before his very eyes? She cocked her head and looked at the adults in turn, then leaned like a bartender on the table. " 'Course, I could play World Cup against Pam on your set at home, for nuthin'."

Pam, mirth dancing across her high cheekbones, made her face deadpan: "You train her to say these things?"

"Absolutely. Start 'em early, sez I."

She made her eyes huge, innocent, and whispered, "Shameless." And then agreed, on condition that they detour to pick up her car at the stadium. As he was peeling off bills for the tab for honest-to-God buffalo steaks and classic Kulmbacher beer, Pam said, "It just occurred to me: you big TV stars have to get up very early. Maybe we should do this another time?"

She was making it easy to disengage—and Jesus, what about Kathleen? Well, screw Kathleen, or rather unscrew her, unless Pam left early. There was no question in his mind about dalliance at his place, not with Laurie there, and he didn't give a damn because this delightful woman affected him like champagne. He wouldn't abandon the bubbles just yet, and as they squeezed into the Genie, he told her the evening was young. He promised himself that he would simply have to call Kathleen later.

Laurie, to his surprise, wanted to ride with Pam. He let her, laughing to himself as he spotted the Honda following him to Hyattsville because now he had a tail who was *really* tail, if he wanted to be raunchy about it. And he did, and he didn't; Pam seemed the kind of forthright good woman who made a man ashamed of his own readiness, but ready nonetheless. Using hand signals, he directed Pam to park behind him at his garage and then walked them to his place, easing into their argument on Great Video Games I Have Known once inside the apartment.

Laurie proved the more knowledgeable player, defeating her father and Pam in turn until Ramsay finally edged her at Pelé. "I'm sleepy, is all," she excused her loss. "Okay if I crash, Dad?"

"You were double-teamed, kid," he said, hugging her and grinning as Pam got a quick hug too. He poured skim milk for them all and took a razzing from Pam on the spartan contents of his refrigerator.

"Next time you raid that fridge, Laurie," she said as

the girl headed for the study, once her own bedroom, "grab a baseball bat for the attack of the mold monster in there."

"Weapons are unAmerican," Laurie recited seriously, and yawned off to bed.

"Now, there goes a well-rounded liberal," Pam said.

"Ten pounds too well-rounded," Ramsay responded. Pam assured him that Laurie would lose her chunkiness, watching him at his coffeemaking game, applauding softly as he managed it in forty-three seconds, closer to the record. "You inspired me," he said. "Maybe there's life after forty, at that."

"Think of years as seasoning. I do," she said. And kissed her fingertip and placed it against the tip of his nose.

If Saturday had worn well, it only improved after late coffee. Pam showed him what happened when marshmallows were briefly microwaved, sprinkling walnuts on the grossly swollen puffs of sweet nothing, enmeshing her small fingers in strands of goo to feed him a bite. He found one edible strand stretching from her lips to his, and they vied for it, and the kiss began with shared merriment but quickly turned solemn. The kisses that followed were sweeter, he said, than warm marshmallow.

"And a whole lot less caloric," she said, her smile faltering. "I don't usually, uh—"

"Fool around," he supplied. He was nuzzling her throat at the time.

"When a woman says that, no one believes it," she said, her hands in his hair, wriggling with pleasure. "Especially when it's true. No, I was going to say I'm not usually one for the fast quip and *toujours gai*."

"I'm not sure I care. But why are you doing it, then?"

"I—guess I didn't expect you to be so uh, compatible, dammit! It scares me a little. A lot. Here I am hiding behind repartee, because it's not as dangerous as honesty but it's not as satisfying, either.'' She thrust her fine breasts against his hands.

Now he was stroking her nipples gently through her blouse, gazing into her face, their open mouths touching as they breathed in unison. He said, "I want to do something with you that is very, very satisfying, if I can get my goddamn couch unfolded."

"So do I, so do I." She crooned it in bittersweet agony. "But I will not do it tonight. Don't look at me like that," she pleaded. "If you have any idea how possessive a young girl can be, you can imagine how Laurie would hate me if she walked in on us. I want her to like me, Alan!"

He had not removed his hands. "This wouldn't bother her?"

With the pleading, a wicked smile. "Kissing she might handle. Fondling, maybe. If we go onto that couch, Alan, I get a triple-X rating."

He let his hands fall away, touched her hair which had fallen to a cascade over her shoulders. "Bitch," he said fondly. "You're right, sure, of course. I want her to like you, too. Shit, hell, damnation. I wanted you for breakfast tomorrow."

"I want you right now. For a midnight snack. And I promise—ah, you meant to have breakfast."

"You'll drive me berserk. Yeah, pancakes, bacon, all that domestic crap."

She drew her hands slowly from his shoulders, letting her formidable nails rake gently down his pectorals, then took his hands in hers. "Nothing could be simpler, but I've got to go now. For the sake of all three of us. I'll be back around midmorning. For breakfast; the three of us. Okay?"

With mingled longing and anticipation, he agreed; helped her collect her things, enjoyed a head-swimmer of a kiss at his front door and listened to the tictac of her

quick footfalls to the sidewalk. Then he steeled himself
for a call to his ex-wife.

Kathleen was an iced vitriol cocktail on the phone, but
accepted his story that he'd been interviewing a woman
and yes, Laurie had been with them constantly.

He put down the kitchen phone extension, wondering if
a bourbon-and-water would make him sleepy enough. The
sooner he slept, the less time he would spend waiting for
Pamela Garza. One helluva day, he decided, was Saturday.
Could Sunday fail to be better?

He seldom remembered, later, how well Sunday began,
with Laurie setting the table and mixing batter while waiting for Pam's arrival; because it all turned to ashes when
he began to scan the Sunday paper.

'Georgetown Savant Succumbs' might have been anyone, but it was Broeck Wintoon. Found by housekeeper,
blah, blah; apparent heart attack at his Chevy Chase house,
blah, blah; history of heart trouble, survived by sons, and
so on; for years a respected figure, decades of service,
author of, *et cetera*. Stunned, Ramsay walked to his study
like an automaton and tried every channel, cursing each
sermon and commercial, then calling his own station.

The paper had it all, evidently. Wintoon's seizure must
have come on Friday evening, some hours after their meeting. Was there any chance that Ramsay's mad scenario
could have brought it on? But hell, the old man had spoken
of cocktails at his club, and a follow-up at leisure. Ramsay
was calling an order for a wreath when Laurie answered
the door buzzer. It was Pam Garza, with a bottle of crack-
ling non-alcoholic cider.

Pam glanced his way and, misreading his face, assumed
guilt. "I've brought some—oh, Alan, did we make a mistake?"

He finished the call, took the bottle from Pam, and
hugged her while Laurie frowned at the mystery. When he

showed them the paper and explained, Pam seemed relieved. "If you'd like to talk, I'm a good listener," she said, starting to share the breakfast chores.

He remained morose until halfway through the pancakes. "I need to talk to somebody," he admitted then, "but I don't want to involve you."

"Let me worry about that, Alan. I'm not a schoolgirl."

Laurie, around a syrupy mouthful: "What's wrong with schoolgirls?"

"Not a thing, honey. But your dad's responsible for you, and I'm responsible for me. Never forget that," she said in Ramsay's direction.

He nodded, realizing that Pam Garza was a woman of great pride and self-confidence. Then he told her of his long friendship with Broeck Wintoon.

Later, while walking off their meal in a nearby park and watching Laurie pump great arcs on a child's swing, Pam remarked, "I'm terribly sorry this man's death hit you so hard."

"It might not have," he sighed, "if I didn't feel that I might've put some stress on him. I picked up an unsubstantiated rumor and asked him about it last Friday. Can't pass it on now. Sorry, but that's the way it is."

"Surely you can't blame yourself for an old man's heart attack!"

"It was the kind of rumor that spreads guilt around," he said glumly.

"Not around you and me," she teased, then saw the long, level look he gave her. "I see; maybe we should talk about something else."

So they ambled back to Laurie and proposed a late lunch. Without spoken agreement, the two adults accepted that theirs was to be a conventional courtship, and that it had already begun. Laurie, to Ramsay's surprise, seemed to accept it without rancor.

Pam left them after lunch and, when dropping Laurie

off, Ramsay had a brief, defensive talk with Kathleen. He niced himself out in that exchange and did not recover his on-camera affability until shortly before the broadcast.

Afterward, he sped home at a pace that risked a ticket, wondering if his answering machine would have a call from Pam. He found her parked at his garage, dozing, listening to music behind the wheel of the red Honda.

Ushering her into his apartment he asked, "Do you realize that I haven't even scrubbed off my makeup or taken off this stupid tie?"

"I shouldn't be so predictable," she purred, and helped him with the tie. Good luck charm or not, she said, that tie had seen better days. But as it turned out, Alan Ramsay had never known a better night.

It had been many years since a young woman had turned Ramsay's priorities upside down, but he could not deny the facts. He did not attend Wintoon's funeral, and begrudged the time spent on his profession. For a few days and nights he suffered the symptoms of a benign disease best known among the young: romantic love.

Most of his waking moments, he felt feverish. He forgot appointments, changed his mouthwash, cleaned his refrigerator out, and bought new shorts. He changed his sheets every morning and Scotchgarded his couch. And every night he and Pam Garza soiled everything again after late, light dinners, playing out their mutual fantasies.

Monday she became his 'casual' pickup in an Ethiopian restaurant in the Adams-Morgan district, but he failed the charade after she asked about Laurie. Tuesday they devoured seafood at the Pompano, later devouring each other on his couch. Wednesday she entered his apartment wearing savage spike heels and, he soon learned, a garter belt in deference to a kink he'd admitted. She wanted him submissive for once, or so she thought, but joyously abandoned the idea after five minutes of satiation with her fully clothed and him dutifully naked. "Some victim you are," she said with a pretend pout. "I don't think you care who's having who."

He agreed, rolling her over. By the time they fell asleep Wednesday night, each knew virtually every sexual provocation that delighted the other, and they spoke fervently of love. Yet, while Pamela Garza could navigate his apartment in the dark, he still had never seen the Washington apartment she shared with another young career woman. He knew everything she wanted him to know, and nothing more.

He did remember to call Laurie Wednesday evening. He would always treasure that call.

Thursday morning at the studios, he signed for a slender package brought by one of the private messenger services so popular in Washington. Those messengers were sometimes slow to deliver but they were very, very private, and they had not received the package in the mail until Tuesday.

Inside the package was a microcassette from Broeck Wintoon. Ramsay locked his cubicle, stuffed the tiny cassette into his pocket memocomp with fingers that shook, and stuck the playback unit's earpiece in his ear before playing the tape.

Over the faint background hiss, Wintoon's voice: "Well, my lad, I just happened across someone who should know about, shall we say, the sinister machinations of Professor Henry Higgins. And I just happened to bring up your little zinger. Amazing what the old-boy net can do. Apparently the elders have heard the rumor, and we both know they have their own lackeys in trenchcoats.

"The rumor is without foundation—I'm almost sorry to say," the voice chuckled. "But of course I'm relieved, really. Otherwise, all weekend I'd be cudgeling this old head over it, instead of enjoying my new Grumman canoe. More likely, I'll be swimming in Deep Creek Lake, depending on how well I remember how to handle a one-man rig.

"My Lord, how I drone on! At any rate, just thought I'd pop this off to you before I leave. By the way, this messenger service is a pretty fair cutout too. Remind me to give you their address. And any time I can help, I'm happy to. Be well."

Ramsay hid his face in his hands during the second playback, half in grief, half in concentration. The old man had loved double entendres and jargon. By 'elders' he meant the National Security Council itself. Evidently his informant had been someone attached to that august group, someone well-entrenched in the pipeline, perhaps CIA.

And the Henry Higgins reference had to be from Shaw's play, *Pygmalion*; the speech teacher who had groomed a student all too well with recording machines—which explained the phrase, 'sinister machinations.' How like Wintoon to discharge a responsibility to a friend, and by a devious route, before charging off to his cabin in western Maryland.

At least, thought Ramsay during his third playback, Broeck Wintoon hadn't sounded edgy or harried. Surely the fatal seizure was not connected with the favor he'd done. Ramsay slipped the microcorder into his pocket and hurried back to the organized bedlam of the studio, leaving one corner of his mind to chew on this message from Broeck Wintoon's grave.

Ramsay was walking off his lunch, watching a frail old woman perform an act of great courage in hurrying across a Washington boulevard, when that tiny mental corner spewed out what he should have realized on Sunday morning. Old Wintoon had set a hot pace up and down those library stairs when an elevator was handy. And canoeing, with a history of heart trouble? Not fucking likely! Wintoon had been a cautious man, and his physical pace would have been plain insanity for a man who knew he had a heart problem. Maybe his heart had stopped, but had the stoppage been natural?

"No, by God," Ramsay said aloud, and hurried back to his office.

He made a spot decision and called the office of General Nels Magnuson from his office phone. Legal fictions aside, joint chiefs weren't all equal but the Army's Magnuson was the only chief Ramsay had ever got drunk with after NATO exercises. Magnuson was not in, but an aide who valued media was happy to help and made the usual promises. Ramsay rang off, pocketed spare microcassettes for his memocomp, and took another walk.

In the mall parking lot fifty yards from the NBN studios, an unmarked utility van resounded faintly with an internal knock. The van driver craned his head to peer back into the gloom. "Got something?"

"He just called a general at the Pentagon, Bobby."

"About what?"

"Wouldn't say, but my stress analyzer says he's climbing walls. The general was out. Do we wait 'til he's in?"

"Christ, no! But call it in, first, Harman. If we move without clearance it's your ass and mine both."

The van thrummed away half a block from where Alan Ramsay sat, the Genie's top sealed as he murmured into his memocomp.

SEVEN

RAMSAY'S REVELATION TOOK UP LESS THAN ONE COM-
plete cassette. He did not refer to Martin or Alden by
name though poor Wintoon could no longer be harmed,
and his name added credibility. Ramsay edited the tape
until, step by step, he built a damning circumstantial case.
Harrison Rand might be simon pure, and Walter Kalvin
an angel of guidance, but some nameless force was ruth-
lessly seeking the carriers of that rumor. If Alan Ramsay
was not already on an erasure list, he expected to get there
soon.

He made a copy of the tape before leaving his car and
hurried back to the studios seeking postage. In each of the
two padded envelopes he placed a tiny cassette with a note:
TO BE MADE PUBLIC IN THE EVENT OF MY
DEATH, DISAPPEARANCE OR DISABILITY, signed
with his legal signature. Luckily he'd entered Alden's address into the memory of his pocket memocomp. It was

not luck but premonition that made him leave his name off the studio's return address.

He entrusted the second envelope to the nightly news producer, cautioning Irv to squirrel it away at home and forget it until the day he, Ramsay, became conspicuously unable to do NBN's work. Irv merely nodded, folded the envelope into an inside coat pocket, and made a wry comment about threats from jealous husbands. Ramsay did not enlighten him; the people Broeck Wintoon had contacted did not seem to deal much in threats.

Ramsay had thought himself calm and controlled for his segment of the evening news, describing the plight of Costa Rican families whose sons fought on the Nicaraguan border while death squads stalked those families. Then, unbidden, his mind flashed: *Holy God, there are death squads nearer than Costa Rica; they could gun down my daughter,* and viewers saw Alan Ramsay struggle through an instant of what seemed to be sudden stagefright. He overcame it with rigid self-control, completed his piece, then ran for the nearest telephone.

He reached Kathleen's recorder and blurted, "Kathleen, you and Laurie could be in terrible danger! For all I know your line is bugged. Grab the kid *now*, right this minute, and, and oh hell, uh, you know where I proposed? Go there and wait for me to page you or meet you! No police; I'll explain later. Listen, Kathleen: if you still have that little snub-nose equalizer, take it with you—*and don't trust any strangers!* I apologize to you both, and I'm sorry for this and, and I'll make it up to you. But do it right now, this instant! 'Bye.''

He rejected several plans while flogging the Genie toward Kathleen's place. He knew where Laurie's key was hidden. Once inside the condo he could reach Kathleen by phone if she was at work. And he would ransack every drawer until he found the little Smith & Wesson she claimed to hate so much. But Ramsay double-parked behind a Metro Police cruiser and, sprinting to the condo, knew he was too late.

Even as he showed his ID to the uniformed cop at the door, he saw past the man's shoulder. Kathleen Ramsay lay sprawled within a neatly taped outline on her living room carpet while a plainclothesman circled her with a video unit. "My daughter," he croaked, ignoring the man's question, then shouting: "Laurie! Laurie, pudd'n! Where's my kid?"

Lieutenant Wayne Corwin, Third District, was a rectangular balding man who dealt well, if brusquely, with stunned citizens. He introduced himself and warned Ramsay against touching the pathetic slender shape that lay face down on the carpet. "The only way you can help her now is to let us do our jobs," he said.

Then he ushered Ramsay away from the protocols of Homicide forensics and into Kathleen's kitchen. Even though Kathleen had fought, there was very little blood. Both of her head wounds, said Corwin, were probably from a silenced twenty-two caliber handgun at point-blank range because no one had heard shots. "Did the victim own such a piece, Mr. Ramsay?"

"I don't think so. A thirty-two revolver, if she still has it. My daughter Laurie: where is she?"

A long studied silence before Corwin said, "We hoped you might tell us. There's no ransom note."

Ramsay slumped against the wall, flooded with weakness and nausea. "Oh God, oh Laurie—" And then he decided that he must be very careful talking to Corwin. He rubbed his hands, which had become icy, and stammered out a hope that Laurie could be somewhere safe.

"I'd like to think so," Corwin sighed, and told Ramsay the worst. Moments after a neighbor heard a woman's screams from the condo, two men had been seen lugging a big plastic garbage can from the condo to a double-parked van. "Unless Mrs. Ramsay owned any heavy art objects? That's a possibility."

Ramsay shook his head. "Can you trace the van?"

There was always hope, said Corwin. "You could help if you have any idea why the girl might be taken. Beside the obvious ransom motive, of course."

For all I know, this guy is a direct pipeline to Laurie's captors, Ramsay thought. Invigorated by anger at the idea, he looked into Corwin's eyes. "In my business you make enemies," he conceded.

"Including ex-wives who have custody?"

Ramsay: "You can go—sorry. Kathleen and I get along. Got along," he amended, and squeezed his eyes shut from the pain of it. "I see Laurie often. Why the hell would I kidnap my own kid?"

"It happens," Corwin said gently. "Then you deny that you and the deceased had recently quarreled over custody?"

"Damn' right I deny it! Oh, sometimes we argued about this weekend or that, or where I took Laurie. My God, be reasonable, I'm not—"

"Homicide and kidnapping in broad daylight aren't reasonable crimes, usually," Corwin interrupted. "I gave you a chance to tell me what happened here. You know, but you're not helping. What am I supposed to think, Mr. Ramsay?"

Whispered: "I don't know." Then more strongly: "I just want my kid back. I'll say anything, or not say anything; whatever it takes to have my daughter safe," Ramsay pleaded.

Corwin rubbed his nose as he studied the distraught father standing before him. "I don't think you set this up deliberately, but you knew you had big trouble before you got here. What kind of trouble?"

Of course, Ramsay thought: *the phone recorder!* "I'm not sure. I've had some—threats, indirect threats, really, and during a telecast today I realized that someone could go after my family instead of coming directly to me."

"But you didn't call nine-one-one and tell us," Corwin persisted.

"I couldn't. I still can't. I left a message for Kathleen so I could—hell, I don't know. Protect them myself, I guess."

Corwin lifted one corner of his mouth without really smiling. "A man wouldn't do brain surgery on his family, but he'll try to do a cop's job." Pause. "Where did you expect to meet them?"

"A scrubby little McDonald's, a couple of miles from here. I figured they could hide in plain sight."

Corwin: "You proposed to your wife at a greasetrap?"

"It was her best proof of my proletarian tastes," Ramsay said, and the two exchanged the wan smiles of men whose wives had never quite housebroken them to elegance.

From that point on, their interchanges became warmer. Corwin agreed that, at this point, publicity could not help Laurie. For that matter, the Metro Police could truthfully say they had no real proof the girl had been abducted. But Ramsay, said Corwin, was no pro at dealing with kidnappers. It was impossible to overstress the importance of getting in touch, and keeping records. The police would be contacting Ramsay again, sorry but police work had its rituals, one being that victims were encouraged to cooperate with the police; was that clear?

When Ramsay moved from the kitchen he saw that Kathleen's body had been removed so quietly, so professionally, he hadn't known when they did it. She belonged to them, now. So did he, if they chose. And Laurie: whose chattel had she become? He seemed to be moving in a very exclusive circle now, in which he alone was an amateur in matters of sudden death.

En route to his apartment, Ramsay began to think clearly

again. Committing a murder, then taking Laurie from a Georgetown condominium during rush hour, was itself a message of power—and of restraint. It would've been simpler just to kill her. And they would kill without hesitation, had perhaps fired two bullets into Kathleen's head for no better reason than to prove it. They'd get in touch with Ramsay to make their demands, no doubt about that. And by this time, they might have taps on his phones at home as well as at the studios. So might the Metropolitan Police—*and they might be working together. I'm bucking the White House,* he thought. Christ, there was almost no limit how wide a net could be cast from 1600 Pennsylvania Avenue!

But the operative word was 'almost.' Ramsay knew a little about electronic bugging, had researched it for telecasts, but thought it unlikely that the National Security Agency's automated monitors would identify him from random phone booths. It might depend on what he said.

He swung the Genie around Logan Circle, shot away and drove to Glenwood Cemetery where he watched for surveillance before doubling back. It seemed that he was not being followed, but perhaps they no longer considered it necessary. With Laurie as bait, they could reel Alan Ramsay in anytime they liked.

He parked at Gallaudet College and got a fistful of change from Student Services, but had to place the call from off-campus. He reached Matthew Alden's home recorder but this time, no friendly voice broke into Ramsay's spiel. "Matt, I'm calling from a public booth. You recognized my voice before but I've got my thumb pressed against my larynx just in case voiceprinters are as good as I hear they are.

"You also said to warn you, just in case. I'm afraid your old friend was onto something incredibly big, and powerful, and it has cost the lives of two people close to me. Maybe three. Maybe me, if they want to. I may be under a magnifying glass, phone taps at home, the best that high-tech can offer. I don't know for sure and I don't want to risk leading anyone to you.

"And my daughter is missing; probably kidnapped. If there is any way on God's earth you can contact your friend for me, do." Momentarily, he was near weeping. "My eleven-year-old girl, Alden; they've killed her mother and I don't dare open up to the police, that's how big this is!"

He took a shaky breath, then several quick ones, and added, "Don't trust anyone on any government payroll, and don't take my word that you're safe. I could've slipped up, somehow. And please, *please,* if you can, tell your friend. I'll give you good odds he's under someone's death sentence, so maybe I could trust him. That's all. Watch your step and your family's." Ramsay was leaving the booth when he remembered he could call from any booth and query his own apartment's message recorder.

He found another booth, called his apartment, punched in the playback signal. Pam Garza had called, suggesting that she cook *antojitos* in his apartment to avoid restaurant food. Some Pentagon staffer of Magnuson's had called to say the general would be out of the area until Monday but would be available at two-thirty that day, if Mr. Ramsay cared to confirm.

And then another call; a harsh unisex voice that had said only, "This is once, Ramsay. Go home."

Finally the same voice calling again, and this time he—more likely, she—was more instructive: "That's twice, mister. We know you can get these calls if you want to. We won't run all over hell calling you from here and there. We'll just start sending you bits and pieces. Go home, Ramsay."

Ramsay made it outside the booth before he vomited, broke a dozen laws getting home, parked in front of his garage to save time, and stormed into his apartment as the telephone began to ring.

It was Pam. "You know what *antojitos* are, mister?"
She was utterly unaware of his panic. "Little delicate mor-
sels you nibble with your teeth. As it happens, I have
some," she said, sensuously teasing.

"Come on over," he said. "I have to keep this line
clear for an important call."

Pam was only half amused. "Important? What am I,
chopped liver?"

All but shouting: "Great, bring chopped liver!"

"You're a very weird man," she said, vexed, and rang
off.

The injection had taken effect fast, but Laurie awoke
very slowly. Her joints hurt, and it was dark. "Mom?" A
flat echo mocked her. She rolled off the bed—no, only a
bedroll on a wooden floor—and padded barefoot toward
the slits of light outlining a door. It opened with a sud-
denness that made her squint.

"Hello, Laurel," said the woman, in a voice that was
barely a woman's. She was not tall but thickset, with short
bangs and a square, wide jaw, and the hands that steered
Laurie into the fluorescent-lit room were terribly strong.
"I'm Johnnie," the woman said, smiling, touching her
breast as if sign language were required.

"I hurt a lot. Where's my mom?" Then, as recent
memories pushed through the fuzziness: "Those men were
hurting my mother!"

"Your mother's all right, Laurel," said Johnnie. "She
said you must hide here with me for awhile. I'm a friend
of hers, you see."

Laurie did not see much that encouraged her. The larger
room sported only collapsible furniture and portable ame-
nities: card table, two chairs, a large cot. A small portable
TV and other equipment lay on the table; magazines
mounded under the cot. Three small fruitwood logs burned
in a glass-fronted fireplace for heat, most of the light com-

ing from a battery-powered fluorescent lamp on the table. No light would get past the heavy drapes, which had been sealed against the walls with broad-headed roofing nails. Opposite the small room where she had slept, Laurie could see through a doorway where a camp stove and canned goods lay strewn across a kitchen countertop.

Laurie studied the woman with the mannish clothes and the stout arms of a bus driver. She wanted to use the telephone. She didn't understand why she was here, and she said so.

Johnnie explained in simple words, the words one might use to a simpleton or a six-year-old. Laurie thought Johnnie's smile might have been baked on until Johnnie claimed that Kathleen Ramsay was in trouble with the police, and Laurie hotly disputed that. Suddenly, in place of the smile, there was only the glittering flat gaze of a pit viper. "Don't call me a liar, Laurel," she said in that voice like something from a cartoon, yet not in the least laughable.

Fists on her hips, Laurie proved she was an only child: "It's Laurie, not Laurel, and I don't know you. If Mom's in trouble, I wanta call my dad. You better get me a telephone or—"

If the red flag was 'you better,' Johnnie was the bull. Wrenched off balance by the woman's thick fingers in her hair, Laurie found herself dragged to a chair. Johnnie pinioned her arms with ease and thrashed her ample bottom. "You—will—behave," Johnnie punctuated some of those heavy slaps. The louder Laurie screamed, the heavier the slaps became until Laurie collapsed, sobbing, bent over Johnnie's lap.

Then Johnnie quit paddling and began kneading, stroking the bruised buttocks, speaking more softly. "Nobody can hear us out here, Laurel. If you behave, I can make you feel good. Real good. *Stop that*," she lashed a single slap again at Laurie's renewed struggle. "You're Johnnie's girl now, and you do as I tell you."

A half-hour later, Johnnie taped the girl's mouth, wrists and ankles securely and locked her in the dark room. Soon after, Laurie heard the sounds of a door closing; a lock snapping. But long before that, while lying across the woman's lap, Laurie had begun to understand and to loathe exactly what it meant to be Johnnie's girl . . .

Ramsay's phone did not ring again until he had greeted Pam and apologized. At first he would only tell her that Laurie had been taken by persons unknown. He said nothing of Kathleen's death, but Pam's lovely dark features remained frozen in horror for many long seconds as she stared, shaking her head. "No, oh no, they couldn't," she moaned. Shaking, she buried her face against his chest.

Touched at her reaction, he said, "We just have to wait and hope." They did not have to wait long.

He answered on the first ring. "You're smart enough to follow orders," said the not-quite-male voice that was now familiar. "Let's see if you're smart enough to keep the girl alive."

"Whatever it takes," Ramsay admitted. "I'll trade myself for her if that's—"

"Shut up and quit trying to keep me on the line. Go right now and check the battery in that yellow sportscar of yours."

"The battery? But—" But he was talking to a dead line. He put the phone down with great care, fighting for self-control, and did not quite hear Pam's question. In any case, she had stammered. He asked her to repeat it.

"I asked you what he said."

A two-beat pause while their gazes locked. Yes, it was natural to assume the caller was male. And it was almost a 'he' voice. But hadn't Pam almost asked 'what did *she* say'? Doubt, as heavy and cold as a fragment of a dead star, came to rest in Ramsay's chest as he turned away from Pam Garza. "He said to check my car battery. Do you suppose they're watching to see if I'll follow orders?"

Pam grabbed her cardigan sweater, tossed his jacket to him, and crossed to the door expectantly. He took the jacket and followed her downstairs, watching the nape of her neck instead of the fine lilt of her racehorse legs. He wondered why Pam Garza had come into his life at this precise juncture; whether she had done it under orders; and then he wondered how he could touch her in pleasure while holding this suspicion.

He let her stand beside him in the driveway while he pulled the inner hood release. She seemed ready to lift the hood herself until he warned her to move far away. If this was a booby trap, at least Pam was unaware of it, he thought. But instead, someone had placed a plastic bag atop his battery. *She probably knew it was safe,* he reflected, holding the clear bag up to study it in the glow of a distant streetlamp, unable to identify its contents.

Hurrying back to his apartment, he said, "They put this here during the past half-hour."

"God, but they're cocksure," Pam said.

He swung the front door shut, ripped off his jacket, folded his arms. "What's your conclusion from that?" He half expected her to say, in awed tones, that his enemies were so all-powerful that he must obey their every whim. In that case he probably would have struck her.

But Pam was emptying the plastic bag herself and did not seem to have heard him. "Oh," she said softly in dismay, handing him the long curl of blonde hair that was Laurie's color but might, after all, have been anyone's. The keyring, however, was more conclusive: its charm was in the tiny spherical magnetic compass. Ramsay had given it to Laurie when she'd gone away to camp the year before. Pam held it up and looked her question silently.

He nodded. "Hers," he said, and took the note as Pam

extracted it. "Until this moment, I never realized I could kill in cold blood. Well, I could. Right now."

From all appearances, Pam did not see the threat as directed at her. "So could I, Alan." She pointed a tapering manicured finger at the folded note as if the paper were a black widow spider. "Tell me if I should see that." Her finger, he noted, was shaking; the skin around her mouth and nostrils was unnaturally pale. *She's not acting,* he realized with a flood of relief and affection. *Whatever she is, Pamela Garza is no kidnapper.*

The note had evidently been printed out on a common pocket memocomp. He read it, paused, then handed it to Pam. Once, while scanning it, she made a noise that was half moan, and the other half was growl. The note read:

WITHOUT YOUR IDLE RUMORS, WINTOON AND THE WOMAN WOULD BE ALIVE. THE GIRL WILL STAY HEALTHY EXACTLY AS LONG AS YOU STAY SILENT. WE COULD SEND OTHER SNIPPETS INSTEAD OF HAIR, AND WE WILL, IF YOU CONFIDE IN POLICE. SOME NIGHTS THE GIRL WILL CALL YOU AT HOME. KEEP YOUR SILENCE AND NORMAL ROUTINES FOR A MONTH AND WE WILL RETURN HER SAFELY.

MAN PROPOSES, GOD DISPOSES.

THINK OF US AS GOD.

Handing Ramsay the note, Pam rubbed gooseflesh from her forearms. "Devils would be more like it. Alan, did they—is Laurie's mother—?"

"Yes. With a handgun. While they were stuffing Laurie into a goddamn garbage can during rush hour today, if you can believe that."

He watched as she traced circles on his carpet with a shoetip, her arms folded so she could grip her elbows. Simply to be doing something, Ramsay went to his kitchen and inventoried the stuff Pam had brought: among other things, soft avocadoes, brown sugar, and lamb chops. She was standing beside him before he finished, and he failed in his effort to smile. They embraced quietly in sexless mutual need. Finally: "If you need to be alone, I can go," she whispered.

He denied it; dared her to create New Mexico *antojitos* that might make him momentarily forget; and watched her small taloned fingers prepare a feast as they talked. The talons paused as he admitted, "For all I knew, you could have been one of them."

She'd thought of that, she said. "I can't blame you; you really haven't known me that long. Just tell me how I can help, Alan, and grade me on how well I do it. But I don't think I want to know those rumors, if they're this deadly."

She took chances, he replied, just being with him. "No, I won't saddle you with what I know. Why don't they just zap me and be done with it?"

She set the microwave oven dial and shrugged as she faced him. "I don't know, but I think we might be safe as long as you don't tell everything on national television. I suspect they're just a little afraid of what might happen if they tried to kill someone in your line of work, and got caught at it. I mean, you're a frequent houseguest to fifty million people, Alan. My big boss likes to say the media is an outlaw horse, you can't tame it, but if you tickle its *cojones* it might give you a good ride. Well, that's what he says," she ended, her cheeks the color of a ripe peach. "Actually, he claims it was a quote from Showers."

"Evan Showers?" His glance was keen. Showers, the President's press secretary, did his job well if unconventionally; just the sort of man needed to run media interference for a President whose public performances were reminiscent of an evangelist.

Pam nodded. "My boss's boss, if the truth be known—and that's just between you and me," she added quickly.

"I thought you worked for Elite Research," he began, and then smiled as she nodded. "Ah; then Showers is one of Elite's clients." The practice of government's hiring independent research groups was not widely known, but increasingly common. "Short-term jobs, or ongoing?"

"Ongoing," she said. "Elite does a lot of what we call unobtrusive measures. You know, computer analysis of talk show jokes, that sort of thing. Subtle measures of how well the administration is doing."

"Pretty sharp of Showers," he said.

"Walter Kalvin, you mean," she replied, opening the oven door. "I gather from little things Tate says and does that Kalvin's the brains behind the stuff we check on."

The sort of subtle details he'd pick up in postgraduate work, Ramsay thought. *Oh yes, Kalvin's had himself a hidden agenda for a long, long time.* "A regular little intelligence service," he said aloud, "if Showers wants it run that way."

She sniffed at the steaming casserole, gave a judicial nod, and placed it on the table. "Elite's first contract was directly through Kalvin; a real internal disaster," she admitted as they sat down. "You know how Harry Rand likes to walk around with a hand-held mike instead of standing behind a lectern with armored glass?"

Ramsay snorted with amusement as he helped himself to fragments of pimiento, lamb, and cheese layered atop corn chips. "It's the preacher in him," he said. "A lot of us think it's as bush-league as Pop Warner ballgames, but it seems to work for him."

"Kalvin wanted a grass-roots opinion before the Presidential campaign," she said. "Tate thought the habit would be a turn-off for a national audience. I'm afraid he cooked our data a little to bolster that opinion," she said ruefully, "but it got harder to cook as time went on. The public just plain liked the President's style and Tate finally had to admit that, or provide outright false data. Don't

you breathe a word of this to anyone, Alan. I'd be in serious trouble.''

"I didn't hear it," he said around a mouthful of deli-
cious cholesterol, pantomiming a feeding frenzy. "You
cook food better than you cook data," he added.

"Oh, I'm what they call a field analyst; what I really
do, mostly, is jolly people into giving us free information.
A lot of legwork," she shrugged.

"You're highly qualified there," he leered, chewing
happily.

"I don't always like what I have to do. But it's for a
good cause," she said. "And where else could I earn
oodles of money, and meet people like Alan Ramsay?"

"There's that. But what's the good cause?"

She colored slightly; busied herself with her fork.
"Harr—President Rand is a fine man. I grant you he's no
genius, but he's a decent person. I've been a supporter
since before he ran for the senate.''

Ramsay lowered his fork. "You're kidding. You were
hardly more than a kid.''

"And he was on the evangelical circuit. I went out of
curiosity and—oh, I suppose you had to be there. To see
him striding across in front of an audience, full of love
and hope and anger and joy for us, it just—I guess it was
something like a religious experience," she said. "For
three thousand people.''

Ramsay began to eat again, nodding, chewing, thinking. "That's a big audience." He saw her nod and went
on, "Did he use a wireless mike then?''

"I don't remem—oh," she said, grinning. "No, the
mike had a cord. He tripped over it once; pulled the jack
out of the socket. I remember because it's the only time I
ever saw Walter Kalvin on his knees, scrambling to fix
it.''

"Probably still experimenting," Ramsay said, aloud but
to himself. Then, snapping his attention to Pam and her

entree, he took another helping. "Quite a coincidence, your getting a job here and finding Rand's people are your clients," he said.

She looked at him steadily. "It was no coincidence. And I'd rather not peer down a gift horse's throat, Alan." They both fell silent, savoring the meal, until Pam said, "Aren't there some things about your job that it would be unprofessional of you to talk about?"

"Not many. Some," he admitted. "Sure; a few."

"Same here. I wouldn't have shared any of this with you, especially considering the work you do, if I weren't sharing everything else with you. There are just some things I mustn't talk about."

"Professionally."

"Yes, professionally. What are you getting at?"

"At the last morsel in this dish," he said, smiling at her abruptly, scraping with his fork.

"You're changing the subject. Finish what you were going to say."

"I'm not sure," he said, "but I know it would involve using your position to help me."

She reached out to touch his wrist gently, her gaze sad and steady. "I have a commitment to you and Laurie now. That's not your decision, it's mine."

They sat in silence while Ramsay considered the ways that Pam might help. It was not conviction but desperation that made him ask, "Pam, if I asked you to deliver a note to Kalvin personally, could you do it?"

After some thought, she nodded. "My career would be on the line if he didn't like it. Tate's my boss, and Showers is in between them," she reminded.

"Just an idea," he sighed. "I'm not sure what I want to say." *If Laurie comes to harm I'll blow you away during a press conference?* Or more likely, *Give me my kid now and I'll retire from the business.* No, his best option for Laurie was to prove tractable, to do as the bastards said and keep quiet for a month. *Why a month?*

He puzzled at that question fruitlessly, staring into space until Pam insinuated her toes between his feet beneath the table. She stroked his calf, smiling, and presently he felt arousal for her—a miracle in these horrendous circumstances.

An hour later, after they had titillated each other through the kitchen cleanup and moved into his bedroom with busy hands, they lay spent on his bed. Perhaps not entirely spent, as she used one languid hand to stroke him to a passable erection. "Ah yes," she murmured, "the potency of the press. Would you say I'm holding the wand of power, love?"

"I'll say anything you like if you promise not to stop."

Her chuckle was salacious in the shadowed room. Then, as they lay together, she whispered into his ear: "You're right, Alan. Don't trust *any*body; not old friends, not even me entirely. But I'd like to know that you've written down everything for posterity, just in case."

Mumbling: "So you can read it?"

"No. Because it might keep you alive."

"I already did," he said, kissing the long curve of her throat. He felt her relax then.

They were half-asleep when the call came. Ramsay bounded into his study, grabbed the phone. "Ramsay here; hello? Hello?"

This time he heard no adult voice, but a series of clatters and clicks and then, unmistakable, Laurie's voice: "Daddy, she wants me to tell you what I saw on the news." Click, pause, click. "There was this story about a train jumping off, uh, derailing." Click, pause, click. "She tapes this so you'll know I'm okay but," click, pause. Click. "I love you, Daddy and Mommy."

He tried to reply but the line went dead. Obviously, someone had taped and deleted some of Laurie's message.

Just as obviously, Laurie could watch NBN's local news-casts. That meant she was within the local coverage area, and she did not sound as if she was badly injured. "Hell, she could be on the other side of Baltimore," he raged.

Pam stood in the doorway, fetchingly disheveled, worry lines robbing her face of youth. He ran his phone recorder playback through its speaker for her; watched while she gnawed her fist in concentration and dismay. "She doesn't know about her mother. They may even have some mercy."

He nodded, sitting at his desk now, laying his cheek against her flank as she moved near. "Maybe it won't be as hellish for Laurie as I thought," he said.

Unspoken between them was the knowledge that his own daily routines were going to be utter and absolute hell.

EIGHT

THE THEATRE IN THE WEST WING'S BASEMENT HAD ORIG-
inally been quite small; scarcely larger than the Cabinet
Room upstairs, dwarfed by the nearby Situation Room with
its communications equipment. The enlarging of the theatre had been Kalvin's idea. The long narrow stage and
the new ranks of plush seats, he had told Harrison Rand,
would give the President the kind of room he needed when
addressing a sizeable group in a private setting.

Standing in the Situation Room with Rand, Kalvin
tucked a gray wand under one arm as he reached up to
straighten his President's tie. *But it won't matter how he
looks if he doesn't follow my script,* Kalvin thought.

Kalvin had spent years trying to account for every sig-
nificant variable which created that public paragon, that
potential monster, the charismatic leader. The Nazis had
one thing bass-ackwards: you didn't begin with the char-
acteristics of the leader, you began with the typical *fol-
lower*. The same voice qualities that hypnotized most

people could generate doubt, or even subconscious hostility, in a few. The chief trick was to find what won over the maximum number of followers—especially in one-person, one-vote democracies where the decisions are made by a majority of meat, and not necessarily a majority of informed opinions. In 1930's Germany, a certain stridency in tone had done wonders. Americans, half a century later, responded better to deep resonances, among other things.

Kalvin had worked long and hard to identify those other things. He had microminiaturized a suitcase full of tubes and wires into a package that fitted into that gray wand under his arm, and finally made the whole thing wireless after a few harrowing accidents. Studying the latest advances in voice stress analysis, which often revealed when a speaker doubted his own truthfulness, Kalvin had added defeat circuits that simply eliminated those tonal tipoffs the stress analyzer was designed to identify. And because Kalvin never entirely trusted Harry Rand or anyone else to follow orders exactly—to stick to the script, as it were—Kalvin slaved the Donnersprache circuits to a wireless enable-disable unit in his own pocket. The instant Rand varied from what Kalvin wanted to hear, Harry Rand became only a regional orator, the mike only an amplifier, the formidable Donnersprache circuits only sleeping sorcery.

And when Kalvin chose to enable those circuits again, then President Harrison Rand's mighty voice flowed through artificial channels to emerge with rhythms and cadences and resonant tones of self-assurance that most listeners found irresistible. *And all he knows is, whenever he deviates from my script, his results are poor. That's powerful reinforcement to a man who wants to be loved,* thought Kalvin. Still holding the wireless mike under his arm, Kalvin tucked the Presidential tie in, nodded at his handiwork—all three-piece-suited, two hundred and thirty pounds of it—and said, "You're letter-perfect on your speech?"

"You know I'm a quick study, Walt. Quit worrying, you just make sure that bunch of congressmen is ready for their minds to be changed."

"I checked the viewport; Showers got them seated a couple of minutes ago," Kalvin replied, and withdrew the wand from his armpit, handing it to the President. "Don't forget your mike."

Rand took it, a device longer than most cordless mikes with a faint patina of use on its knurling from Presidential palms after all this time. "Look, I don't need this thing for forty or fifty people," he said. "I know folks kid me about my old-fashioned delivery. Might not hurt to modernize my image a little."

"It would ruin you," Kalvin said, understating the truth. "Anyhow, you need amplifiers in a room that size."

"So why not use a smaller room?"

"Because then you couldn't use your own special style. Peripatetic, remember?"

"Walkin' around while you talk. Aristotle. Sure I remember, but if I didn't do it, I wouldn't have to use this thing," he said, shaking the microphone like a party noisemaker.

"Please don't do that," Kalvin said quickly, reaching out to the wand. "You could bang it against something. Wouldn't want to damage your lucky mike."

"*Your* lucky mike," Rand corrected. "You're the one who got all pale and sweaty that time in Atlanta when I—"

"My lucky mike, then." Kalvin had invented that explanation years before after his own nervous near-collapse when Rand, speaking live at a Georgia fundraiser, mislaid the device that had taken Kalvin years to develop from its ancient German prototype. They had found it in the pocket of a janitor, an hour later. "Humor me, Harry. It's part of you by now and we don't want to change a winning combination."

They began to walk to the reinforced doors, a staffer opening a door smartly, getting a nod from the President. As the two men walked down the hall toward the theatre, Rand tucked the wand into an inside coat pocket sewn especially for this use. "How many representatives you think will change their minds from this little chitchat, Walt?"

"Never possible to say exactly; they're a cynical lot, but you could swing half of this group, maybe twenty, if you do it like this in a controlled situation."

"More than one-on-one by phone?"

Kalvin knew that the magic of Donnersprache depended on excellent fidelity, and you could not depend on the fidelity of someone else's telephone receiver. It often worked, but you could not depend on it working well enough, often enough. "Trust me, Harry; this is better. Brings out the old charisma," he said, patting the President's arm, opening the door for his usual informal, bigger-than-life entrance.

Walter Kalvin watched the reaction of forty congressional representatives, each summoned because he opposed the new Federal Media Council, each beginning to slip beneath the spell of the moment, each impressed with his own importance, having been summoned to such a friendly confrontation by the President of the United States. A position of highly visible power, Kalvin knew, carried its own magic.

No one noticed when Walter Kalvin sat down, hands jammed in pockets, in a last-row seat. That was the way Kalvin liked it. He toyed with the memocomp in his right-hand pocket, paying close attention to Harry Rand some of the time but to forty congressmen most of the time. Harry was right, Kalvin thought, he was as quick to learn his lines as most professional actors. It would not be necessary to press the special buttons that could remotely en-

able or disable the mike's Donnersprache circuits, at least
not until after the sermon. Actually, the only times Kalvin
needed to disable those circuits was when Harry Rand
took it on himself to cajole or bluster his way into a position that put him in opposition to Kalvin himself. When
that happened, the circuits got disabled.

And so did President Harrison Rand's credibility, without the invisible, silent thunder of Donnersprache.

Kalvin watched and listened as Harry Rand strode across
the slender raised stage, thinking that the man had never
been in better form. Videotapes of the audience response
would tell him more later. And of course, there would be
another such meeting with an assortment of the opposing
members of the Senate. It was all going according to plan,
Kalvin decided. They might not have to eliminate anybody
else, not even that guy Ramsay.

At least, not until after the Federal Media Council became reality. Then they could ice the bastard, him and
anybody else they chose, because even if a killing went
wrong, the screwup wouldn't be a problem unless it became news. And nothing would be news if Walter Kalvin,
chairman of that council, said it must not be news.

NINE

THE ABUSES OF LAURIE RAMSAY WERE MANY, THOUGH most were no worse than a slap. It was the sexual abuse that would leave invisible scars. The worst part of it, Laurie found, was the cloying, sickening pleasure she felt for brief moments in Johnnie's hands. Forced to rely on her own strengths far more than ever before—even at summer camp—the girl made great use of subtlety.

Johnnie kept treating her like a little kid? Very well, Laurie would take tiny revenges by acting the part. In the phrase of Laurie's school chums: sandbag the bitch. Cold water was the only amenity of the kitchen and bathroom, and Laurie's chores included dishes. Spilling detergent, knocking the propane stove into the sink, and clumsiness to the point of idiocy became Laurie's tricks. She quickly learned that she had no hope of moving the heavy drapes away from the clerestory windows, even in the kitchen: the process was noisy and Johnnie's hearing was good. The sounds from outside included birds and occasional aircraft, but no car traffic. Though Laurie was never permitted to climb up and glance out, Johnnie pulled the drapes aside for natural light during the days, performed indifferently as cook, and meted out swift punishment for 'accidents.'

Johnnie's weapons were open-handed slaps and viselike pinches. Two things seemed to provoke Johnnie to attack the girl sexually, and Laurie soon learned the ugly pattern. One thing was any behavior that enraged the woman enough to spank. The other was binding Laurie's wrists, ankles, and mouth with adhesive tape prior to Johnnie's nightly disappearances. When Johnnie returned, she seemed tempted by Laurie's helplessness. And always, after the despised caresses, Johnnie would reward herself with tequila. The woman had brought two quarts of the stuff and gulped it straight from the bottle.

Laurie came to think of sex as horrid punishment, but in analyzing her captivity she also found real wisdom. It was clear that Johnnie had a child's ethic: full attention to what was due *to* her, little attention to what was due *from* her. If Laurie could be forced to do every chore, and to make no demands while Johnnie filled her days with TV and magazines, then Johnnie would not fill Laurie's days with so much anguish.

And one more thing entered Laurie's thoughts: weapons. If anything convertible to a weapon was bad, then Johnnie's hands should be confiscated. Laurie wished she could bring a bottle of tequila down on her captor's skull—which proved that Laurie's hands were potentially 'bad' too. And wasn't Laurie's deliberate clumsiness really a weapon? It was, in fact, Laurie's only weapon. Laurie began to wish she had a better one, something with which to defend herself against power both illegal and immoral.

Laurie had begun to question the tenets of pacifism. And to consider alternatives, and then to busy herself with empty food containers which, in camp, she'd learned to make into a tea set.

Johnnie saw her small captive making 'cake' from fire-place ash, and brewing 'tea' in metal cans, and Johnnie returned to her magazines with a shrug. Let the little bastard play childish games, she seemed to think, so long as she was obedient and neat about it. Johnnie did not seem to care that, for the silent, intent Laurie, it was more than a game.

TEN

FOR RAMSAY, THE FIRST FEW DAYS OF LAURIE'S CAPTIVITY became a challenge to sanity. He canceled the appointment with Magnuson, fully aware that he was choosing Laurie over the future of his country. He found anodyne in his work, driving himself in solemn intensity, telling himself that 'they' would return Laurie in a month—and not believing it.

Incredibly, not even the scrofulous tabloid press penetrated the cone of silence around the death of Kathleen Ramsay, which was duly announced by Lieutenant Corwin as "suffered in her Georgetown home during a break-in attempt." Aside from a few of Kathleen's friends who had never liked Ramsay and did not intend to start now, Ramsay noted that Corwin and two of his men were virtually the only others to attend Kathleen's funeral. "What's really galling," Ramsay said to Corwin later, as they walked between rows of headstones, "is that she was bright, useful, a good mother. And she's been put away without a ripple of suspicion anywhere."

"Put it in plain terms, Ramsay: you mean she's gone, and her murderers are running loose," Corwin corrected. "That's what happens when the people who could help us, won't."

"Sure; I talk to you, and they kill Laurie by inches." Strain made his voice tight, almost shrill. "She calls me every night, Corwin, did you know that?"

Corwin knew. Did Ramsay know that the calls came from different directions? Arlington, Silver Spring, Cheverly. Audio analysis suggested that Laurie's messages were first sent from some single location as scrambled transmissions over ordinary phone lines, to telephone booths spaced around the Washington area. Then someone would call Ramsay and play the tape. The calls were never long enough for police to fix the exact location.

"All the earmarks of very, very organized crime," Corwin said. "Maybe politically organized. If you said the right things, Mr. Ramsay, I could bring in the Feds. But I won't force you."

If Corwin was part of it, he was role-playing and the hell with him. If he wasn't, maybe he could be pushed back to arm's length. Ramsay asked, "What if it's some lunatic group of the Feds themselves?"

After a moment: "If—mind you, that's an 'if' I have seen only rarely in seventeen years—but if it were, I could accidentally drop you and your daughter into deep shit. But I don't like this, either." He jerked a thumb back toward Kathleen's grave.

"I have to protect Laurie. She's all I have, now," said Ramsay. Corwin's sigh and shrug implied understanding, and Ramsay's suspicions of the man dropped a notch. The rest of that day, Alan Ramsay debated himself over courses of action, and ended by choosing inaction.

Each night, Ramsay waited with Pam Garza for what

had become both low and high points of his day: Laurie's
call. On Thursday, perhaps intending to frighten him, his
enemies made a serious mistake: they did not make that
call. He slept little that night, and on Friday morning he
gave every appearance of settling down, resuming business as usual, accepting the facts. But while lugging his
video equipment across town, he made the call he should
have made earlier.

He'd intended to send another mayday to Matthew Alden. But Alden's answering service clicked to an intercept
an instant after Ramsay began to talk.

The voice was not Alden's. "Take down this number
and call from public booths until you get an answer." The
number had a local prefix with a three-zero-one area code.
Bethesda? He punched the number into his memocomp
and decided to keep his interview appointment before
making the next call. Five minutes after a deadly dull interview for NBN, he found another phone booth as though
at random, blood pounding in his ears.

Two rings. Then a man's voice, a drawl more West than
South. "Mr. R., modern gadgets are so good they can be
tipped off by a name or a key word, and they focus on that
call."

"I know that, but—"

The voice went on, interrupting him. Recorded. "Think
very carefully before you speak and avoid key words or
names, especially your own. If I like your replies to the
following questions, stay on the line." Pause. "Who introduced you last night on the defense appropriations piece;
and what kind of tires did you buy for your little Chevy?"

Instantly he said, "Ynga Lindermann gave my lead-in,
and it's not a Chevy as you probably know, it's a Genie
with wide Pirellis."

A click, and now the voice was live, the same measured
gravelly baritone on the recording. "Good enough, Mr.

R. I was wondering if you had the smarts to call Mr. A.
again. I see you did.''

"I hope I haven't put him in the same bind I'm in,"
Ramsay replied.

"Not as long as you keep calling from different anonymous places. Your home phone is bugged two ways, conventionally by Metro Police and by less friendly people
using small transmitters. Your office lines aren't secure
either. You must continue to use a different booth each
time you call me. And for the moment, you must talk as
if you were wearing a bug on your clothes or even in your
hair—because you very well may be. Their equipment isn't
good enough to hear through your earpiece, though. Do
you understand?''

"Very handy for you," he said with anger he hoped
sounded genuine. If he were bugged personally, they
would only be hearing his end of the conversation. "NBN
has deadlines, you know. So how am I supposed to check
your side of the issue?''

A snort that could have been amusement. "Very quick,
Mr. R. As for my side of the issue, consider me a very
biased observer. Biased in your favor—and you'll just have
to take a chance on us. Think about this: I alerted you to
the problem with a letter. I've got a new name—again,"
the man sighed affably in his first show of human frailty.
"The other side would never offer you any help, even false
hope, because they want you hopeless and docile. And we
don't.''

"That makes sense. But what can you offer?''

"First thing, we get you deloused," the man said
briskly.

"Why d'you say I'm, ah, lousy?" But he felt like
scratching himself all over. Even the idea of an electronic
bug made him feel defiled, somehow.

"Just a hunch; quit talking and listen. Before your next
call, buy a Mantis, it's a sophisticated bug-catcher from

CCI. Branches in Manhattan and Washington. Use cash, not credit card; and even if someone you know has one, don't borrow one, you could be borrowing trouble. Don't tell anyone, not even your best girl, that you have it. Okay?''

"Yeah, I've heard of the firm."

"The people you're up against can afford to bug every pair of skivvies you own. Bugs may look like fuzzy weed seeds. They stick to things. You can wash them out of body hair so they get to listen to the plumbing. Launder them from clothes the same way without raising suspicion. If you find one elsewhere, let it alone. They pick up sounds about as well as your ears do. Still follow me?''

"I think so, but how do I use the hardware?"

"Wear it like a wristwatch; it is one, for that matter. But it pokes you when it gets near an active device, so you can even spot a video bug and it won't know you've tumbled unless you do something stupid like taking the Mantis off your wrist and waving it like a flashlight. And I'm afraid we've talked long enough.''

Ramsay was giddy from all the cloak-and-dagger orientation, and this man had given him no real promise of help. "No, wait, dammit. I don't want to, uh, interview those people. I might be seen. Why can't you provide the evidence yourself?''

"When your mail is monitored? Nope; bad idea. But you have a point.'' After the briefest of pauses, as if to himself: "Sure, why not? If this one goes down the wrong way, we won't be using drops anymore. Call again. Give me ten minutes.'' And the line was suddenly dead.

Ramsay walked out of that booth feeling an almost feverish anticipation, reminding himself not to smile or whistle because it might register on some long lens or tape recorder. Ten minutes later, he had found another booth. "It's me again. You remember what I wanted?''

"Yep. You'll find joy in the Rexall on Connecticut Ave,

a few blocks from where you work. Early this evening, you'll decide your watch is on the blink. Within ten minutes after seven P.M., go into the Rexall. Ask the clerk, *not* the pharmacist and not the cashier but the clerk, for a Timex. Pay him, put it on, and leave. For God's sake don't ask him to demonstrate it, he wouldn't anyhow. Anyway, I suspect this'll be one of your better bargains, pal. But patriotism is the bargain *we* get.''

"The truth is, I'm starting to lose that.''

"Bullshit. You called this number.''

"For selfish reasons,'' Ramsay said, self-disgust flavoring his words.

"I think I know that reason. People in law enforcement sometimes talk with old friends,'' the man said. "Well, you can play someone else's game, or you can keep me advised. If you don't call within twenty-four hours we'll take it as a turndown, and no hard feelings.''

Ramsay thanked him and replaced the receiver, striding out to Independence Avenue feeling as though he should sprint. The man had made no promises but by God, he seemed to be part of something carefully organized. Maybe that, he decided, was what put the vinegar back in him: the man was a total stranger, but he represented hope. Ramsay saw no gleam of it in any other direction.

He made his deadlines at the studio, complained that his Seiko had developed cardiac arrest, and called his own apartment knowing that Pam would play the message back—and that others would hear it. Running late, he said, thanks to a screwed-up wristwatch, and he'd be home by eight or so.

At exactly five after seven by his flawless Seiko, he walked into the Rexall. The clerk was a wiry dark-haired man in his thirties, an inch or so less than six feet, who fitted his surroundings like Tums and aspirin. He was glad to help and my, but that face seemed familiar. Ramsay admitted his name, kept his casual role, and asked to see something reliable in a watch; maybe a Timex?

With nary a wink or nudge, the clerk produced two Longines and an electronic Timex. Ramsay studied each. The clerk remained maddeningly offhanded and made no suggestions. Ramsay turned the Timex over. "The price of this one?"

"You're in luck. This one's a closeout at thirty-nine ninety-five. Something to do with all those special functions," the clerk replied.

Ramsay realized again that he might actually be carrying a tiny transmitter on himself. "I'll take the Timex," he said, and paid cash.

The clerk made change, smiled, and said to the retreating Ramsay, "I expect it's one of your better bargains." Ramsay, with the discomfort of a man who has inexplicably wandered into a staged play, hurried out.

The damned thing seemed to be an ordinary Timex, if you ignored the tiny bar that lay flat on its underside. He slipped it on, thrust the Seiko into his glove compartment, and drove home while aiming the new watch at various parts of his body. Either he was free of bugs, or the watch was faulty. Too bad he couldn't show it to Pam. Odd, he thought, that it could make him feel so much better when, so far, all it had told him was the correct time.

Because Pam was waiting for him at his apartment, he made no overt effort to check the place for monitors, but soon realized the Mantis worked because it gently poked him several times while he was in the kitchen. He felt a surge of anger about that, but knew a fierce elation as well.

When Pam left his apartment the next mornng, he began to use the Mantis with great care. The thing was highly directional in its ability to pick up signals from an active transmitter.

He found the first bug, after a puzzling fifteen minutes,

in a crack of cabinetry between his dishwasher and countertop. It lay very near his kitchen phone. He found the
second one faster by marching directly to the study and
waving his wrist near the desk phone. The tiny device
looked more like a furry tick than a seed, and had been
planted in the center of one of Laurie's 'forever' poppies.
It had lain in full view, had heard every word spoken in
his study, for—how long? Had the bastards bugged him
even before Laurie's kidnap?

Now his elation was gone. A gradually building feroc-
ity, held in careful check, was all that remained. It did not
diminish much during his workday, and he sought a pay
phone soon after lunch. The recorded message suggested
he call after three P.M. and at one minute after, by his
bargain Timex, he called again.

The westerner came on-line immediately. "Did you find
anything of interest, Mr. R.?"

"Damn' right. Nothing on me personally, but I found
two little gadgets near my home phones. God *damn* these
people, I've never even seen them!"

"Oh, you've seen one of them, all right. We're monitoring your little hotsy, Mr. R. I don't know how long
you've known Miz G., but she's working for the other
side. That's why I suggested checking your body. She
probably carries more bugs than Typhoid Mary."

The briefest silence before a gritted, "I'll kill her. . . ."

"They'd love that," said the man. "She thinks she's a
patriotic American keeping tabs on a man who needs
watching, and I doubt you could prove otherwise to her.
If it's any consolation, we gather she's sick over your, um,
babysitting arrangements. Her chief sin seems to be naive-
te. Keep playing her game, but don't let her lead you into
any dark alleys; it's possible they could change their game
plan about you."

"Look, I don't give a shit about *my* hide anymore. If

my kid were safe, I'd blow this whole thing in the media and take the consequences.''

"Not yet!'' The reply was instant; explosive. "Eventually that's just what we'd like to see but these people have a timetable and we still aren't sure why. And if you hurt them too soon, they'd hurt you back a lot worse. And you'd blow *our* show.''

Ramsay, with sudden suspicion: "And what is your show, pal?''

"It's still called the United States of America, I believe. If we're patient, it may stay that way.''

Ramsay grunted assent and changed his tack. "I had a call today from a lieutenant in the Metro Police. He admits they're monitoring my phone. Whose side are those guys on?''

"Yours, apparently, but they can't help much. And if they get lucky, it could be bad news for your daughter.''

"What are the chances I'll see her alive again?'' He hated to ask. He *had* to ask.

"About fifty-fifty,'' said the westerner. "Getting better as they keep her longer and get more confident. Your lady friend's contacts must be through her job because she's not getting them at her apartment. With luck, we just might be able to backtrack those calls. If we can, someone may lead us to your little girl.''

"Is that really one of your priorities?''

A moment's pause, and now something in the man's tone became less commanding, more intimate; sadder, perhaps. "There's an old Greek physician's code that says, 'first, do no harm,' '' he said. "That little girl's troubles began with a decision of ours. We're ethically bound to help free her, you have to believe that. No, you don't have to, do you?'' Those last few words had been spoken as if Ramsay himself had already answered.

"I think you're starting to see how I feel,'' Ramsay said.

"I don't blame you, but I can't do much about—"

"Hell you can't. I do a lot of legwork on my own, pal, and I meet lots of people; informants, interviews, that sort of thing. Why not meet me face to face?"

Now the man's tones were plainly apologetic. "Because if somebody gets you in a spot with needles under your fingernails, the less you know, the better. But your point is taken. Meanwhile, remember: if we do get your daughter back, the instant the bad guys know it, they'll be trying to nail you before you can get to a TV studio. I don't want you to have any false hopes about that."

"The only hopes I have are pinned on an eleven-year-old pacifist, pal. I won't see her for a month, they said."

"A month? Exactly? Why a month?"

"I don't know," Ramsay said. "I hoped you might."

"Maybe we do need a sit-down, Mr. R. But this call has already gone on too long. Get back to me; and stay friendly with your hotsy, but keep checking yourself for bugs, okay?"

"Right," Ramsay answered, and hung up, now more perplexed than before. His allies seemed as curious about that one-month time span as he was.

ELEVEN

At dusk, ten days after the kidnapping, Robert Lathrop parked his rumbling old Firebird two blocks from the suburban home of his real boss, set its alarm, locked the door, and tugged at the vest of his gray three piece suit before walking smartly away with his attache case. In his vest pocket were cards that introduced him, truthfully, as a salesman of household computers. Beneath the vest and the silk shirt was a gut as hard and flat as Nautilus machines could make it, with the help of steroids. If challenged, Lathrop could have produced brochures from the attache case, and pocket memocomps at very attractive prices. Lathrop made most of his money that way, letting his fine physique, those moist brown eyes and the well-scrubbed fresh features do much of the selling for him.

But Bobby Lathrop did not think of that as his 'real' job. His real job put a small submachine gun in his hands, and put him back into the kind of power that a police internal affairs investigation had taken him out of, years before. No police commissioner can afford a disarming, glib young sociopath in the ranks, if he knows about it; especially a bright one. The kind of man who *can* afford a Lathrop is the kind whose budget can be fudged, and who has ways of learning when a Bobby Lathrop has been found and bounced. Such a man had found Lathrop. Bobby's smile, as he skipped up the front steps of Terence Unruh's home, was unforced.

The door opened for him and Bobby strode in, with a dazzling smile for Unruh who seemed, in the dim light of an unlit living room, much older than he had been a week before. "Take a seat, Bobby. Beer? Iced tea?"

"Nothing, thanks. Mind if I smoke?"

"It hardly matters now," Unruh said, and sank carefully into an overstuffed chair near Bobby. "Quit looking around; my wife and the kids are at a school play. We're secure."

Bobby, with the highest respect for Unruh's security sense, visibly relaxed, pulling a set of pages from his case before he lit the Winston. "Transcripts from Ramsay's phone."

Unruh took them. "Any other copies?"

"No, *sir*," Bobby assured him, grinning again. "Jondahl's tape transcriptions are there too. Johnnie's as steady as a bitch wolf."

"Bitch wolves aren't queer for pups," said Unruh.

Bobby's jaw twitched. It had been a mistake to tell Terence Unruh so much about the habits of Johnnie, beyond her dependability, and doubly a mistake to crack explicit jokes about the Ramsay kid's captivity. "Well, Reba Jondahl can't be charmed by kids and she won't balk at stringent measures," said Bobby. "When we're this short-handed, we're lucky to have somebody like Johnnie that we can depend on."

After a pause, tiredly: "I suppose."

Bobby thought the phrase, sighed like that as if by a

defeated man, out of character for Unruh. But Unruh *looked* out of character, as if the thankless job of government—whichever part of it he really represented—had finally caught up with him, aging him a year for every week. *No wonder he keeps the lights off,* Bobby thought. "If you want things simplified," Bobby said, and paused to make his cigarette glow, "let me get creative with Ramsay. Household accidents kill a lot of people, Terence."

"Ramsay has almost certainly written down what he knows and put it in a safe deposit box," Unruh said, his voice soft, lacking vitality. "We want him just the way he is."

"Indefinitely? Why?"

"A month. And I don't know exactly why, Bobby. I just follow orders."

"But if I intercept anything that says Ramsay's going to spill something big—is the sanction still good?"

"Of course," said Unruh. "Just don't hurt that bimbo, Garza, in the process. Someone very high up wants her healthy."

"Small wonder," Bobby Lathrop snickered, and flexed his arms. "I could use her healthy myself."

Another sigh from Unruh. "I'm sure you could. Which reminds me: if Ramsay goes down for whatever reason, at that moment there's no longer any reason for Reba Jondahl to keep the girl. Get the girl away from that crazy butch immediately after that. Is that clear?"

"Yessir," Bobby said quickly, brightly. He saw no point in adding that Johnnie, whom he had busted when he was in uniform and had gotten to know better since, was far more valuable than any snot-nosed kid. Johnnie's features and voice were much too distinctive for even the dullest child to forget or confuse with anyone else. Therefore, the Ramsay kid would be 'taken away' by Johnnie's own hands, just as Bobby Lathrop had already promised the woman. He would simply report the girl missing.

Bobby spent only five more minutes in the Unruh home, accepting a well-used bundle of cash and swapping his phone scrambler attachment for another. It was important, Unruh insisted, that the Garza woman keep Bobby advised on her movements. There was no telling when she might need new instructions from Bobby, and Unruh was hardly in a position to contact her himself because, for one thing, she had never heard of Unruh.

Bobby left feeling that, for some reason, Terence Unruh did not want him to linger. Almost, Bobby thought, as if he was unwelcome in the Unruh home. That was okay with Bobby, so long as their job relationship remained. Other people might fret over friendships. Not Bobby.

No, *sir*.

That night Laurie thought she was caught, for sure. She had let another batch of her play-tea percolate into the tin can she used as a teapot, and poured it into the cup she'd made from a smaller can. Johnnie had turned off the lamp to save its batteries so that the only light came from the fireplace and the little TV the woman was watching. Then, as she'd done several times before, Laurie moved to the raised hearth and slid the half-filled cup past the glass front and near glowing coals.

But Johnnie was watching. "What the hell're you doing?"

Laurie jerked, then covered her guilty motion by sticking two fingers in her mouth. "Nuthin'. You made me burn myself," she mumbled.

"Don't tell me 'nothing,' Laurel." Johnnie stood up and left the TV to stare at the tin cup. "What's that?"

Now Laurie cowered in real fear—but she often did, with good reason. "I'm, uh, I was just boiling tea."

Johnnie squatted at the hearth, squinting into the heat, and saw the clear 'tea' begin to boil around the cup's edge. Then, as Laurie stared, the woman grasped the cup by the

neatly bent metal handle, with scorched adhesive tape
Laurie had salvaged to cover the sharp metal edges. Suspiciously, Johnnie swirled the contents. Then, suddenly,
she spilled some of it onto live coals and moved back as
if expecting a sudden flareup.

"It's just play tea," Laurie said as the coals hissed.

"Uh-huh. Thought it might be cooking oil," Johnnie
said, the threat implicit, watching steam hiss from the
coals. Without another word, Johnnie returned to the TV
and Laurie repositioned the cup. Soon it would be time
for the nightly news, and then for Laurie's report on it.

Presently, after most of the water had boiled away, Laurie's trembling fingers retrieved the cup. She moved back
to her pathetic little tea set and began to slurp noisily. Not
the stuff she had been percolating through wood ash and
then boiled down, of course, but the other cup with plain
cold water. Laurie had learned more at camp than mere
basic woodcraft.

She'd learned how settlers made soap, too.

TWELVE

THE SMITHSONIAN'S AIR AND SPACE MUSEUM SEEMED AN odd place, Ramsay thought, for his first meeting with an ally. But below those huge exhibits, where historic aircraft hung like the predatory toys of giants, sprawled a basement where a man could get lost, assuming he was allowed down there. Ramsay had to show his ID twice before he could descend into those depths, and consulted his memocomp after taking a wrong turn.

He found the door labeled FILM ARCHIVES at last, walked through with his video equipment, and greeted a graying woman whose smile was at first perfunctory, but widened as she recognized his face. She checked his credentials anyway. "It's very unusual, but you're cleared into the archives," she told him. "That makes two at once. *Very* unusual," she muttered again to herself as she ushered Ramsay into a tomblike space with multiple aisles stretching away between ceiling-high shelves. He saw the man with the ancient can of sixteen millimeter film immediately, but the man did not look up until the door had closed.

As the man turned, Ramsay's first impression was of a swarthy farm hand in expensive slacks, perhaps part mestizo; straight longish black hair, prominent cheeks, corded forearms sticking out from half-rolled sleeves and, in a jarring note, gossamer white nylon gloves. He stood and extended a hand, seeing Ramsay's gaze on the gloves. "Just protective coloration, Mr. Ramsay," he said as they shook hands, and Ramsay recognized the voice. "This old nitrate film is delicate stuff. People dart in here every so often, but it's as secure as a missile silo. Remarkable what you can do with the right lodge handshake, isn't it? Call me Tom; Tom Cusick; but if you're more comfortable with a name you know, make it Cody Martin. Both street names." Cusick had a face that could smile and squint at the same time, as though sharing a joke with someone a mile away.

"I'm Alan, or Al if you want to bug me," Ramsay said, and took the vacant chair. "Speaking of bugs, I'm clean." He brandished the wrist with the false Timex. "And thanks. Forgive me for coming right to the point, but anything new on my daughter?"

"No; sorry." A one beat pause. "We have a probable contact, maybe a second, but I can't talk about that yet. If you get picked up by the wrong folks, Alan, *you* can't talk about it. Even though they could make you want to very, very badly."

"Trying to scare me?"

"Yes. If you're already scared, good, and I'll lay off."

"I am. Scared enough that I'm thinking about buying a gun."

Cusick cocked his head, and his gaze was skeptical. "We can't help you there. It's not something we do."

"What, exactly, *do* you do, Tom?"

His hands idly coiling the old black and white film as

he replied, Cusick said, "Most people think of lodge brothers as grown children who raise money for charities. True, as far as it goes, Alan. Did you know that nearly every President, until recently, has been a member of some Masonic order?" Seeing the curiosity in Ramsay's face, he went on: "We try to break no laws, but we'll operate in the chinks between laws."

Because Ramsay had seen the grotesque ways in which honest folk had been co-opted by a LaRouche or a Kalvin, his question was pointed. "Party affiliation?"

"None. Personally, I'm a radical centrist; I'd love to see some profound changes, some liberal, some conservative. It's really not an important question. What's important is this Donnersprache thing that Undersecretary Parker called a charisma device. It might somehow be used to help human beings, but in the wrong hands—well, there might have been a *fuehrer* in Germany without it, but maybe not. And Donnersprache is obviously not in good hands the second time around. Think of us as a few armchair sociologists, Alan, working up a list of the unpleasant things that might happen within, say, a month."

"I've pared my list down to one," said Ramsay. "I don't envision it as a factor on the foreign policy side. And you can put it down to my media bias, but the thing I see fast approaching is a Congressional vote on that damned Federal Media Council."

Cusick had a good poker face, and he was using it. "What if it passes?"

Ramsay shrugged. "Maybe nothing much. Might depend on who chairs it, and how they interpret their clout. Eventually it could be a Supreme Court issue, but the court moves slowly. A hell of a lot of censorship could come down the pike before that."

Cusick nodded. "I don't suppose you have any ideas about exactly how Donnersprache works, or what it is," he said, stirring the air with one daintily gloved hand.

"Yeah, I do. Pretty obvious, once you research Walter Kalvin's background—and Rand's," Ramsay said. "You've researched Kalvin. His degrees; the way Rand's career went into high gear after he and Kalvin got together; all that stuff?"

Another nod. "An interesting view," said Cusick, noncommittal; maybe too much so.

"I don't know how many people are in on the Donnersprache idea, but I think it could be Kalvin's alone. I'm sure Rand knows, of course."

"You are? I for one am amazed at the things our President doesn't know," said Tom Cusick. "And at the things Kalvin does know."

"Like how to build that goddamned Donnersprache gizmo into a hand-held mike," Ramsay said. "I'd love to get my hands on one. I'm sure he has a fucking drawer full of 'em."

"For the record, Alan, I think you're fantasizing."

Ramsay grinned. "But off the record?"

Cusick's button-dark eyes were hard as he shook his head. "Under enough duress, everything goes on record. I can't give you anything that isn't for the record."

Ramsay's hand slapped the table with blinding speed, but without great impact. "What the hell *can* you give me, then?"

Tom Cusick's reaction was quick; a defensive motion with both arms, just as quickly relaxed. "Easy, friend. Pretty quick hands, by the way; I like it. Let's talk about something else," he said abruptly. "We aren't as well-heeled as we'd like, but foresight and the right handshake can sometimes beat money. What if worst came to worst, and you needed to—what we used to call exfiltrate?"

Ramsay frowned, then made a connection. "Disappear, you mean? False ID, that sort of thing?"

A nod. "Don't think it can't happen. I've needed it to keep my head screwed on more than once," Cusick reminded him. "Or maybe just a safe house for a few days. Most of that, we can do. What we won't do," his smile was wry and lopsided as he waggled a hand like a listing boat, "others can, and we can point you in the right direction."

Ramsay needed a moment before making a troubled headshake. "I'll keep it in mind, but that's not my style. And it presupposes that something has happened to Laurie."

"Not at all. It just supposes someone decides to take you out. You're the one who's dangerous, not your little girl. And if you decide you need to run for it, call me. If you get the answering machine, whistle the highest, steadiest pitch you can for as long as you can; it's an alert signal. You *can* whistle?"

"Yeah. Look, why the hell don't you just contact some other media people? A dozen of 'em; somebody not connected to me. Then Laurie would no longer be—oh, my God," he said, seeing Cusick's lowered head, and its slow negative shake. "When she's no longer important, you're saying I won't get her back."

"I'm wishing I could tell you otherwise," Cusick said. "I realize now that we should've broken this to a dozen people simultaneously. But we didn't, we chose you."

"Some favor," said Ramsay, his jaw twitching.

"Some favor," Cusick echoed.

THIRTEEN

TRANSCRIPT OF CONVERSATION FROM
PERSONAL FILES OF TERENCE L. UNRUH
(BY SUBPOENA; UNDATED):

U: Go to Beta scrambler, please.

K: Wait a minute. Okay, on my mark: mark. (BRIEF LINE INTERFERENCE)

U: Kalvin, something's wrong with Ramsay.

K: (LAUGHS) There's supposed to be.

U: No, I mean he's not behaving right. He's been trying to talk back to those messages from his daughter, and I've recorded it for analysis. The stress analyzer showed he was climbing the walls. Now he's not.

K: Don't expect him to stay at panic stress levels forever, Unruh. Take my word for it, he should level off at medium to high arousal.

U: Well, he did. But he dropped off that plateau a couple of days ago.

K: Not too surprising if, uh, he's probably taking downers. That would figure, and you could verify it with Garza, I imagine.

U: I had Bobby Lathrop ask her about that. She says not, but Bobby is worried about her dependability. I'm not new on a stress analyzer, Kalvin, and I tell you the man is psyched up, wired. I don't know—

K: If that's all that's bothering you, see to it that his kid is crying in tonight's call. Must I think of everything?

U: You'd better, and one thing you'd best think about is just how long you can keep a man like Ramsay on the edge of a nervous breakdown. If he blows his top, Christ knows what he might say, and I don't have enough men to assault a mental ward.

K: Two weeks, Unruh, two lousy frigging weeks. I trusted you to recruit all the assets you needed.

U: Look, I'm, uh, just sending you a flare. There's something going on in Ramsay's head and if it's a short fuse to a blowup, you could be lookin' at that fast flight to Quebec.

K: We covered that a long time ago, Terry. You said my exfiltration was all in place.

U: It is. But it's not exactly your favorite scenario, is it?

K: I was just asking; it won't be needed. Not ever, if everything goes as it's tracking now. You just take care of your assets and I'll take care of mine. Uh, how are you doing? Personally, I mean.

U: Am I still dying, you mean. (LAUGHS) I'll last more

than two weeks, asshole. I intend to stick around long enough to see what comes from all this.

K: In the meantime, if you're right, you'll need to run tighter surveillance on Ramsay.

U: I'm spending several hours a day getting treatments, Kalvin. I can't be expected—

K: Just handle it.

U: You're all heart. (LINE INTERFERENCE. MESSAGE ENDS.)

FOURTEEN

LAURIE KNEW THE AGENDA ALL TOO WELL. JOHNNIE never skipped more than one night in making Laurie describe the news, and she had skipped the previous night. So, later tonight, Laurie would be tightly bound again for Johnnie's foray outside and when she returned the hated demonvoice would form obscenities while the hands and mouth performed worse obscenities and at last Johnnie would drink her tequila. Laurie felt her lip curl. She knew her teeth were showing; she did not recognize it as a smile.

Johnnie switched TV programs on a precise time schedule according to the small comm set by the TV, its digital readout relentlessly counting off the last hours of life. The compact Sony unit was clearly more than a recorder with earphones and clock because once or twice a day, at no predictable intervals, it would emit a series of thin chirps. Immediately, Johnnie would punch a code into the calculator. Laurie had earned a slap for watching the woman operate that pocket comm set. Laurie had realized that the chirps were incoming queries. Johnnie's coded response told someone, somewhere, that all was well.

Johnnie would not ignore that signal merely because it woke her in the night, as sometimes happened. The outstanding virtue of Reba Jondahl was her passion for obedience—whether she was master or servitor. Laurie Ramsay had come to understand this central pillar of Johnnie's existence. Because they were short-handed, Bobby Lathrop could not afford sloppy work and rejoiced to have someone like the Jondahl woman who, ex-con or not, kept highly dependable routines.

Now Laurie, too, joined in that rejoicing. Exactly on time as always, Johnnie went to the bathroom carrying her heavy purse and the comm set. Laurie sat against a bare wall where she could watch the TV. And as usual for the past few days, the girl seemed to be dozing, her blonde head on her knees. Laurie knew how to create a routine, too.

Laurie kept her breathing steady until the bathroom door closed, knowing that she must complete her stealthy work within two minutes or so. She moved quickly, terrified at small sounds; the pop of her joints, the clink of utensils. She had replaced everything and was near Johnnie's cot, with its supply of magazines and bottles beneath, when Johnnie emerged too soon from the bathroom.

Neither of them moved for a moment. Then, "Going somewhere?" from Johnnie in a snarled parody of sweetness.

Laurie, trembling too hard to speak, could only shake her head.

Johnnie deposited her purse and comm set on the card table, then reached toward the cowering girl. "Thought I wasn't watching," she rasped, prying at Laurie's balled fists and finding them empty of contraband. "Thought you could play fuckaround with Johnnie," she went on, ripping at the pockets of Laurie's filthy jumper.

Laurie's denials made no difference. She took two heavy slaps across her face, tried to protect her head with her hands, then fell to the floor and submitted, sobbing, to Johnnie's body search. That was what made the difference, for the woman found a child's handful of corn chip fragments and a small ball of used adhesive tape in Laurie's pockets.

Johnnie, breathing hard, tossed the ball of tape into the fireplace and surveyed the sad little hoard of food fragments she had scattered to the floor. "Clean up that shit," she commanded, assuring that Laurie saw the mess by grasping the girl's hair and shaking her head above it. Then Johnnie seated herself at the table and found a TV sitcom, watching occasionally as Laurie, on hands and knees, carefully removed specks of food and cast them into the fireplace.

At last the job was complete. "Don't do that again," Johnnie warned. Laurie sensed that the woman did not know what 'that' had been. And through her sniffles, behind her cowering as she slumped down against the baseboard, Laurie knew it would not be necessary to do it again.

Laurie saw her dad on the nightly news, and thought that he looked older. At Johnnie's command, she duly recited to the comm set about the pileup on the Anacostia Bridge. When she added, "And Johnnie beat me up for nothing," she collected another slap. She did not know whether that accusation would reach her father. She did know it would make Johnnie mad as hell.

To make matters worse, when Johnnie brought the adhesive tape from her purse the procedure became a struggle. Johnnie always hurried to lock up for her brief absences. The woman was brutally efficient, dragging Laurie to her pallet and locking her in. Presently, Laurie heard the outside door lock and, weeping from fresh bruises, she fell asleep. She knew that she would soon be awakened.

Johnnie's return, and her sick attentions to Laurie, were routines the girl suffered with a sort of ghastly anticipation. This time Johnnie carried her to the cot, removing the tape from her ankles but leaving her wrists and mouth taped.

After ten minutes Johnnie sat on the edge of the cot, her drives assuaged. "Starting to like it," she accused, in that notwoman voice Laurie had come to equate with Satan's. "In prison, you develop a taste for a lot of things. But not the stinkin' chock," she said with her coarse-grind laugh, bringing the tequila bottle from under the cot. "You make chock from cornmeal, sugar, raisins, yeast, anything you can get on the inside. Always tasted like shit to me. Not like this," she added, unstoppering the bottle.

She turned and smiled down, staring into the girl's eyes that, despite the tears, stared back. "This Sauza is good stuff," she confided, swirling the remaining few ounces of nearly clear liquid, and then took a triumphant swig.

Johnnie swallowed over an ounce before the gag reflex closed her windpipe. It had taken Laurie Ramsay over two weeks to collect and evaporate the stuff, percolated through wood ash, that became four ounces of a primary ingredient of old-time soap: concentrated caustic lye. It had taken her less than two minutes to substitute it for tequila. It took Johnnie only seconds to realize that the lining of her throat was gone.

Johnnie blinked as she flung the bottle aside, but not fast enough to prevent a splash of lye into her eyes. She leaped to her feet, convulsed with an agony that spread from her throat and face into her belly, then wheeled back to the cot. Reba Jondahl had known from the first that she would have her choice of ways to kill the girl, and had already decided on slow strangulation. Now, even deeper than the fiery pulse in her guts, one intent burned in her brain: to reach the girl's throat. Johnnie, half-blinded and unable to breathe, reached down with both hands.

Wrists still bound behind her, Laurie saw it all, just as she had hoped, and knew what those callused claws were seeking. Lying on her back with knees flexed, Laurie used her left leg to push off and swept her right leg up with every ounce of fury an eleven-year-old soccer jock could muster. Laurie's kick was awkward but her sturdy legs were driven by desperation. Her right heel caught Johnnie precisely on the jawline, full force.

The woman spun on her left foot; crashed against the card table; fell face-down as the table knelt, spilling the lamp and TV set onto her body. Reba Jondahl was aflame from inside and her ruined throat would not permit the passage of enough air. Rolling onto her back, mouth wide, she began to claw at her own face.

Laurie rolled from the cot in mortal terror and leaped to her feet. She had not expected Johnnie to recover and she knew that, if her hands were not free soon, the woman would certainly kill her.

The tape on her wrists would not yield. She knelt at the raised hearth, her back toward it, and began to worry the tape against the abrasive edges of bricks.

Even though her mucous membranes were slowly being flayed alive, Johnnie somehow began to manage a hoarse whistle of breath. Semiconscious, she rolled over, staring through her agony. She was clinically blind by this time but she could see the girl's vague shape facing her. And her lungs seemed on the verge of getting enough air. On hands and knees, carrying an inferno in her body, Johnnie lurched in Laurie's direction, paced by the whistling rasp of her breath.

Laurie kept sawing at the bricks until the last possible instant, then scrambled up, and her sidewinder kick took Johnnie across the bridge of the nose, snapping her head hard enough to make her hair fly outward. Johnnie fell on her side but, instead of continuing to kick, Laurie ran to the bathroom. Perhaps, she thought wildly, she could slam the door for more precious seconds of life. But her clothing caught on the latch striker plate protruding from the door facing, and the rip gave Laurie new hope. She worked to catch the frayed tape against the little tongue of brass, moaning with terror because she could see Johnnie come up on hands and knees again, blood runneling from her nose.

Then Laurie felt the tape begin to yield, caught at it with desperate fingers, tore harder against the brass plate heedless of the pain at her wrists. When two layers of tape wore through, perspiration helped her slide from the rest. Laurie, tearing away the strips at her mouth, slammed herself into the bathroom.

Which had no exit.

The only light was from the crack under the door, and Laurie knew that the devil herself would soon be at that door, obscuring all of her light forever, and when Laurie wrenched the door open again Johnnie stood almost erect, leaning in the hallway, wiping at her eyes and making that dreadful hoarse gasping noise. It was not so much courage as horrified panic that sent Laurie bolting past, her arms windmilling furiously, her small body slamming past Johnnie to sprawl into the big room in the half-light of the lamp on the floor.

There in full view lay Johnnie's big purse, open, with a small holster clipped inside it. Laurie fumbled the dead-black thing with the thick handle out of the purse and turned to face her pursuer. She had never heard of a Heckler & Koch P7, but she knew it was an automatic pistol. And even a child could see that sighting was no more complicated than alignment of two white dots in the rear with one white dot in front.

Johnnie may have thought that Laurie was only threatening, holding the H&K at a range of two paces. That was because Laurie's hands were small and initially, even with a two-handed grip, she was not fully depressing the squeeze-cocker safety. When Laurie finally succeeded, Johnnie's opinion was revised by a thunderous noise and a single nine-millimeter round just above Johnnie's navel. The woman doubled over as though lashed by an invisible foot, then sat down hard in a way that would have been comical in other circumstances and slowly fell on her side.

Laurie had never fired a weapon and, unprepared for the sound and recoil, dropped the pistol. By the time she recovered it, Johnnie half-lay on the floor, face contorted, fumbling with the little comm set as she tried to operate it blindly.

Laurie knew that the woman was in hideous agony, and that Johnnie was in some ways not quite human. And she also knew what you were supposed to do with animals in hopeless pain. Buoyed by this rationale she found it easy, with the muzzle an inch behind Johnnie's skull, to squeeze the trigger once more.

What erupted from the other side of Johnnie's head was not stuff Laurie wanted to remember, as Johnnie jerked and flopped like something filled with dirt and did not move again. But as Laurie laid the weapon down and emptied the purse onto the floor, the ringing in her ears became a chirping too. Then Laurie realized that the chirps were not inside her head. They were coming from the comm set.

Bobby Lathrop enjoyed tooling the Firebird around, even if its brakes were lousy, and he took the Gaithersburg turn-off from Highway 70 by gearing down so that Harman, his companion, grabbed for a handhold. Jondahl's failure to respond was probably just an equipment failure, the two men agreed. It would take a half-hour to actually reach the isolated house by road, and only moments to rectify the trouble. So much the better; neither of the men en-

joyed the company of that reptilian twat, though that wasn't
supposed to count among hardened pros. After parking
near the darkened country place, Bobby stayed at the wheel
while Harman, wearing the thinnest of leather gloves, took
his stubby Ingram stuttergun into the house on recon.

Harman came back at a dead run. "Somebody's plucked
the kid," he panted. "They whacked Johndahl, man, I
mean *recently!* Still warm. All her fucking credit cards and
shit spread around—but I didn't see that little shooter she
carries. And listen, I want you to come verify something."

Bobby flowed out of the Firebird fast. Harman's obser-
vation was easy to verify, but not to figure. If some rescue
team had got past Johnnie, then why the fuck would they
unscrew the hinges of the back door from the inside, leaving the combo lock untampered?

Not once did Bobby or Harman entertain the idea that
an eleven-year-old child, sufficiently brutalized, might have
managed such carnage unaided. . . .

FIFTEEN

RAMSAY PADDED INTO HIS STUDY AND ANSWERED THE phone as churlishly as anyone would, at one o'clock in the morning. "Uh, jus'aminute. . . . Okay, I'll tell her if I see her." He disconnected, yawned from his study into the bedroom playing out the old-fashioned phone cord to its full length, flicked on the light and gently shook Pam's shoulder. "Somebody named Carol Heaton; friend of yours. You're supposed to call forward. That's all she said, tell you to call forward."

Two blinks, and suddenly Pam was wide awake, nodding. He handed the instrument to her, then sat on the edge of the bed.

Without hesitation, Pam Garza dialed a number. "I'm here," she said. Pause. "Yes, he is. In the next room. . . . Of course I am, you should know that by now." Ramsay could hear, very faintly, the timbre of the voice, and it was male. Ten seconds later, he saw the color drain from her face. She pulled the sheet up to cover her, gooseflesh prominent on her arms. "I, I don't think so, I'm not—that's not the kind of thing I—please, no!" Now her free hand covered her brow, fingers unconsciously flexing in her dark hair. She was trembling.

Then, chewing her underlip as she listened, Pam seemed to regain some composure. Twisting the mouthpiece away, her ear still against the earpiece, she whispered to Ramsay: "Get dressed just as fast as you can." Now she resumed talking. "I don't know what I can do, but I'll try," and so on, furiously waving Ramsay away from the bed.

Three minutes later, as he was pulling his shoes on, she put the phone down and fairly leaped from the bed to begin dressing. Her voice was very small: "Alan, Jesu Maria, darling, what have you *done*?"

"You tell me. Where the hell are we going?"

"Different directions. I have to ask where you're going, but you mustn't tell me." She pulled a mascara brush from her purse; showed him the hollow needle that slid from its stem. "I was told this was for me, if I ever needed to use it. But now Lathrop says it's for you. I—even for my country, Alan, you know I couldn't, and I told him so. He must be desperate to even say it indirectly; the police probably heard every word. Then he said to keep you here any way I can until they can talk to you."

He barked a bitter laugh. "I can imagine the questions: bang, bang, and bang. Who the hell is Lathrop?"

"The man I work for, when I'm not doing company business. You don't seem very surprised."

"I'm not. I've known you were on the wrong side for some time." A new thought twisted his face into something ugly. "I don't suppose I could beat you into telling me where Laurie is."

With whispered intensity: "Softly, Alan, there are audio transmitters in the apartment. You must believe me, I had no idea—well, if I knew where Laurie was, I'd tell you. It's just not right! Have you done something so terrible?'' Now she was tucking her blouse in, following him as he headed for the living room closet for a windbreaker.

"Yes. I learned how, without being elected, a man can become the real President of the United States using a psalm-singing figurehead as his puppet."

"I don't understand." Now they were both whispering with quiet fury. "Harry Rand isn't—that can't be true."

He reached for the doorknob. "If it isn't, people are dying over an empty rumor."

She stood transfixed, staring at him, perhaps hoping to see duplicity in his eyes. Then she said, "Look out for Lathrop, he's a bad one. I'm supposed to try and stop you."

In his rage, without a real opponent he could reach with his bare hands, he said the most vicious thing he could: "You'll think of something, you Mexican whore."

She swallowed, taking two steps toward him, tears beginning to course down her face. "Make it look good. Hit me."

He had already turned away in disgust when she said it another way. "If you ever loved me, Alan, hit me."

He wheeled and struck her with his open hand, then started down the stairs as she fell. He heard his telephone begin to ring and did not give a damn.

Laurie had considered flagging down the car—in daylight she would have seen that it was an old Firebird—as it swung into view, half a mile from the solitary house. But she was cutting across an open field at the time, toward the vague glow of neon in the distance. The purse was heavy with the weapon, and the coins and bills were more money than she had ever had at one time. The contents of that purse gave Laurie a heady sense of power.

A small aircraft, its landing lights arrowing past her, swung into its final approach. When Laurie saw the beacon flash across her quadrant of sky, she turned in its direction. That is why, as the Firebird roared back through the silent neon-lit center of Emory Grove, Bobby Lathrop did not catch her.

Laurie made it afoot to the Montgomery County Airpark nearly two hours later, hoping someone there might have a telephone. The man in the old leather jacket was nice, though inquisitive as a truant officer when he saw the swollen left side of her face; but since she only asked to call her mother, he could hardly complain.

But when she dialed home, a recording said that the number was not in service or had been disconnected. Laurie knew that had to be crazy, but she called her dad next.

The line was busy. "I bet he's talking to Mom," Laurie said, and accepted half a Hershey bar from the man, who said he had a girl just about Laurie's size and he would sure as heck like to know how come she was tarryhooting around the countryside at one A.M. He did not seem particularly satisfied by Laurie's shrugged, "I got lost."

Two minutes later, Laurie tried again and became puzzled immediately. "Who? This is Laurie. You know: Laurie Ramsay? Pam? Hi, Pam. Boy, have I had a day, I'm at the airport—" She listened for long moments, ignoring the interested frown of Mr. Leatherjacket. Then: "Well jeez, why not? . . . I don't get it; *who's* listening? . . . Okay, if you say so."

Momentarily, Laurie wore a frown too. Then she said, "Hey, you been crying? Me, too. Huh? Naw, I won't have to hitch, I can take a taxi, I've got money, hundreds and hundreds. And a gun, too." She glanced at Mr. Leatherjacket and saw the gold caps gleaming in his rear molars.

He snapped his mouth shut and began to chuckle as she went on: "Mostly I'm just sleepy, but Johnnie beat me up a lot and," she flushed, catching the man's gaze, "other stuff. Pam, is it okay to kill people like her?" A shorter pause. "Soon as I can. Will Mom and Dad be there?"

She was not pleased with the response and laid the receiver down with, "Durn. She hung up on me."

"Young lady," said Mr. Leatherjacket, "let me congratulate you on the most creative imagination I ever saw or heard of. Can you really afford a taxi home?"

Laurie assured him that she could. "But I'm not going home. And he better take me where I say," she hinted darkly, hugging the purse.

The man said she could depend on it. Herb, the only driver on duty thereabouts this time of night, was a personal friend.

Ramsay couldn't say why he turned the Genie back for a single run past his apartment; but slowing to stare toward the lighted place, he saw the dark Firebird double-parked, one man dashing up the stairs. As Ramsay passed, the man at the Firebird's wheel turned and saw him, then honked several quick blasts. The man on the stairs turned, something squarish and metallic showing through the opening of his coat, and then he was racing back as the Firebird's engine coughed a warning rumble. The driver was hammering on his steering wheel in frustration as he waited for his companion and Ramsay whacked the gear lever, reaching with two fingers for the boost switch on the lever's side. He wasn't sure the Genie's booster was working until his Pirellis began to smoke.

SIXTEEN

HE TOOK THE FIRST RIGHT-HANDER HE SAW, THINKING
that the Genie's maneuverability might make up for a Firebird's monstrous rush up through its gears, and for his own
lack of experience in life-or-death driving. With a ten-
second head start, Ramsay hoped to make enough tight
turns that sooner or later, the Firebird's driver would begin
to lose more precious seconds wondering which way he
had turned.

But Ramsay soon found himself overmatched. Instead
of beginning each turn at the intersection, as he did, the
big muscle car was starting its turns efficiently, very early
and very wide, ticking the edges of curbs, booming down
suburban streets with a surge of sound that Ramsay could
hear above the wail of his own smaller engine. And when
he divided his attention between the streets ahead and the
onrushing Pontiac behind, he managed to misjudge his
own path. The big car loomed only five seconds behind
when Ramsay, driving beyond his capacity to react to what

appeared in his headlights, saw the extreme dip at one intersection too late to avoid it.

He braked in panic when he should have accelerated, the Genie's nose diving, rebounding with a mighty thump of bottomed suspension, starting a sidelong slide. He released the brake, judging that if he was very, very lucky, the Genie might make it between a fence and a brick wall into someone's driveway—which meant that, lucky or not, he would be afoot within seconds.

Except that it was not a driveway at all. He had turned in at an alley, a piece of Americana left over from times when trash collectors drove behind a house, not past its front. Ramsay nudged the edge of the fence with his left front fender as he powered past it, still badly overdriving his lights. He saw a streetlamp's glow a hundred yards ahead, then squinted into his rearview at the twin beams that caught him as the Firebird entered the same alleyway. But the Firebird, still jouncing from that dip in the intersection, had too much weight to recover its poise in such a short distance. It missed the fence but evidently not the brick wall, and then Ramsay caught a glimpse of orange sparks showering an outline of the big car, still pursuing but now with only one headlight.

Someone had left a huge pile of trimmings—leaves, grass and small branches—against a back fence on the right side, and Ramsay slowed just enough to steer to the left of the mess, brambles screeching down the left side of the Genie as he slammed his foot on the accelerator again. His right wheels, whirling through the edge of the trimmings, bounced hard and then he was past them, risking another look back. The drum and wail of his Genie were too loud now for him to hear anything else, but he saw winks of light stutter from the Firebird as if signaling.

Signal, my fat ass, he's shooting, Ramsay thought as his outside rearview mirror exploded three feet from his face. Then the Firebird driver elected to force his way straight through the trimmings. Ramsay had never seen a car stop so fast in his life.

Below all the grass and leaves lay cordwood, piled in no particular order, flying forward into the Firebird's single headlight beam as the car became a bludgeon. Ramsay did not realize until he was turning left onto the paved street that the Firebird was rocking backward, then forward, as lights began to wink on in bedrooms that flanked the alley.

Ramsay took a right, then another right, then a third, simply because it seemed the last thing his pursuers would expect. As he flashed back past the street where he had exited the alley, he spotted the Firebird lit by a streetlight, turning left as he had done, its entire right side a ruin, dragging its rear bumper. Before he passed from sight, he saw the big car's nose dip under heavy braking and assumed he'd been seen. He took the next right-hand alleyway he found and got a two-second view of a weedy track that was clear as far as the next street. He shut off his lights and continued much more slowly, letting his eyes get accustomed to the light of stars and half a moon, snarling, "Yeahhh," with a raised fist when the Firebird hurtled up the street, crossing behind him, the bellow of its engine rising as it kept accelerating. Somewhere in the distance, sirens hooted.

He proceeded down the alley for two more blocks, using his lights only for brief flashes, and turned right onto a paved street after making certain that no headlights were approaching from any direction. After a few blocks, he turned his lights on and headed for Route 1 and the District of Columbia.

He parked as inconspicuously as possible behind a Seven-Eleven, still trembling, and wondered if his panic flight had condemned Laurie to death. He tried to tell himself that they would keep her as a bargaining chip as long as he maintained his silence, but he remained uncon-

vinced as he entered the phone kiosk and consulted his
memocomp. Ten seconds later he began to whistle a single
tone into the mouthpiece, a tone as shaky as he was.

He tried another tone less wavering, and when someone
lifted the receiver he said, "You called me Mr. C., and
you offered me a place to hide. Well, I need it. I'm in
trouble."

Someone told him to wait. He waited a hell of a long
time, it seemed, before he heard the sleep-fogged voice of
Tom Cusick. "Understand you need a safe place. What
happened?"

Ramsay told him. "Maybe I should've stayed," he
added, "for my daughter's sake."

"You did right," said Cusick. "Something forced them
to change plans; something major, I think. We'll work on
it. Right now, let's get you picked up. And your rolling
toy that anybody can spot a mile off, we'll need to hide
that. Um; you know where we met? You arrange a breakdown on the street outside. Can you get there in thirty
minutes?"

"Hell, I can do better than—" Ramsay began. He was
only ten minutes from the Smithsonian.

"Just yes or no, and I make that yes. Try not to get
there ahead of time." Suddenly Ramsay was monitoring
a dead line.

He bought a cup of coffee in the Seven-Eleven and
browsed among magazines as he sipped. Then he drove
the Genie toward Jefferson Drive, taking it slowly, pulling
to the curb near the massive Air and Space Museum with
three minutes to spare. A tow truck pulled up behind him
two minutes later, three men shuffling from the big vehicle. One of them was Cusick, who pointed at the elevated
cab and told Ramsay to stay in it. One minute later they
had a huge opaque tarp bundled around the Genie; in two

more, the Genie's front end swung gently from a cable sling and the truck was underway again.

Ramsay finished his account as they drove across the Anacostia River into Fairmont Heights, Tom Cusick asking a few questions in the interim. Neither of the other men broke their silence until Ramsay asked, "Why do we need my car, if it's such a giveaway?"

"That's why," rumbled the driver; "bait, if they really want you."

"He can park it at the NBN studios," Cusick said.

"But not too near the building, just in case," the third man said. "And what if they're waiting?"

"We'll run interference with this rig until Ramsay's inside the building," Cusick replied. "But right now, I could use a few hours' sleep."

"God, I'm too wired for that," said Ramsay, but he was wrong. Minutes after they parked the tow truck and filed into the boarded-up service station off East Capitol Street, Alan Ramsay was snoring lustily on an air mattress.

Ramsay was up by seven and tooling the Genie toward NBN by eight, in the shadow of a big tow truck that just happened to turn in abreast of him and loomed so near that parking was difficult. He hurried upstairs and absorbed the impact of a different and more familiar reality, as if the outside world were only a hallucination. He sifted through a stack of callback requests, including one from Lieutenant Corwin that only said, 'We have your girl,' and he wondered why Pam Garza had gone to the cops until he was arguing about a feature with Irv, and then he made the connection that had been too good to imagine the first time around, and he leaped for Irv's phone so abruptly that the producer ducked.

He talked his way past two people before Corwin came

on-line. "Corwin, this is Alan Ramsay. Which girl do you mean?"

Gruffly, but pleased: "How many kids do you have, Ramsay? Laurie, of course." At Ramsay's whoop, which drove the harried producer from his own office, Corwin went on, "She called your place and talked to your lady friend, who told her to take a taxi direct to me, and not to budge out of the cop shop without me. She showed up in the middle of the night at Fourth District HQ in a *taxi*, f'God's sake, with somebody's money and somebody's purse and somebody's gun, and it seems she's whacked out some troll who needed whacking the worst way, but it still sounds very much like homicide to me, but not in my district, thank you very much, and—are you getting this, Ramsay?"

"Where the hell is my daughter right now," Ramsay asked, too stunned by this goofy recital to fully believe it all.

"With me, actually. She tells me you play tricks with coffee makers, is that true? Ramsay? Hello?"

But Ramsay was already running for the exit.

The utility van bore a legend on its side, now, with peel-off block lettering: 'REVIVACAR,' and in smaller letters, '24 hr. service.' The man in white overalls had opened the hood of the Plymouth next to the yellow Genie, and jumper cables coiled on the macadam nearby. Had the Plymouth's owner showed up, it would have been simple for Bobby Lathrop to claim he'd made an honest mistake.

Twice, Bobby stiffened, ducking his head into the Plymouth's innards as mall patrons walked past, but no one seemed curious about his work.

The second man was harder to spot because only his feet protruded from beneath the nose of the Genie. His explanation might have been more creative. Harman worked silently under the Genie while Bobby kept a nervous watch, and when he was finished he slid out with very special care. "Switched on," he said, scrambling into the van.

Bobby lowered the Plymouth's hood, retrieved the jumper cables, and hummed an old tune as he drove away. The tune was "Smoke Gets In Your Eyes."

A hundred yards distant, a tow truck driver picked up his all-band unit. "You have your rabbit, Athos?"

"Hippity-hop, Porthos. By the way, I made one of those scufflers, knew him from the old days. He's got my leash on him but it won't activate for an hour. I'll give him lots of room. Aramis, proceed south on New Hampshire. And be careful, Porthos, you wouldn't want to make a report to the nation."

"Didn't know you cared. Porthos out." Tom Cusick put the comm set down, sighed, and drove the tow truck behind the Genie, taking a small toolkit and an astonishingly heavy blanket as he stepped down from the cab. If worst came to worst, the truck would intercept most of the debris and working from the Kevlar blanket, he might lose only his arms.

SEVENTEEN

ALAN RAMSAY LAUGHED WITH TEARS RUNNING DOWN HIS cheeks, holding Laurie to him, inhaling her scent as she hugged him back. "Boy, could you ever use a bath," he said.

"She wouldn't let me. Oh, Dad, is it true about Mom?"

"Some jackass told her, Ramsay; sorry," said Corwin, who stood by.

" 'Fraid so, pudd'n," Ramsay nodded, and held Laurie again as she broke out in fresh sobs. "I miss her too. We'll get 'em, wait and see."

"Montgomery County mounties found the house an hour ago," Corwin put in. "Laurie got one of 'em herself, Christ knows how."

"I told you how," Laurie sniffled. "I'm not sorry."

"I don't suppose you'd be averse to making a statement, now that it's over," Corwin said to Ramsay.

"Fine, when it's over," Ramsay said, "but it isn't over."

"I could keep you here," Corwin said. It did not sound much like a threat.

Ramsay lowered his daughter to the floor, one arm still draped protectively around her shoulders. "At first I didn't know where you stood; I mean the police. You—look, can I talk to you where nobody will tape us? Privileged conversation?"

"Right. Not legally privileged, I can't give you that. But I can use my judgment. Come with me," he said, turning. Ramsay took Laurie along. It wasn't so much that he wanted her to hear it; merely that he did not want to let her out of his sight.

". . . Supposed to stay in the studios, Ramsay," said Tom Cusick, calling shortly before noon. "When the receptionist told me to call some police lieutenant I thought someone had nailed you. Why are you—?"

"My daughter escaped last night," Ramsay interrupted. "She wound up with the police and I came straight here by taxi. Maybe that's why Kalvin's people were changing plans. Anybody who calls me at NBN gets referred to this number."

A sigh of relief from Cusick. "That's the break we needed. You really have the girl there with you?"

"Sleeping like a lamb; she had a busy night," said Ramsay.

"Then maybe we can step up the pace. I suppose the police are tracing this call, and I'd rather keep a low profile."

Ramsay glanced across at Corwin, who was using an extension. Corwin, smiling, shook his head. "Lieutenant Corwin is on the extension; he says not. Anyway, why would you care?"

"Because I've broken some laws by not waiting for the so-called proper authorities. Disarmed a half-pound of plastique under your car chassis two hours ago. Mercury switch, so it'd detonate when you backed out or hit a bump."

"Lieutenant Corwin here," Corwin broke in. "Have you notified the Alcohol, Tobacco and Firearms people?"

"No, I just took the detonator out of the circuit and left the damned thing where it was, on the front suspension crossmember. You might get some good prints off the device; but not mine. And two friends of mine are smooth-tailing the guy who seems to be running this piece of the operation."

"All we need is a bunch of amateurs," Corwin began.

"Professionals. Retired, but not all that retired," Cusick said dryly. "You want to take it over?"

"There are some things they can't take over," Ramsay put in. "But I have a contact who could start from the other end. At the top."

"That's dangerous," said Cusick. "Kalvin's thugs are almost certainly some part of the intelligence community."

"We're wasting time," said Corwin. "I have enough facts to start on, but a set of prints on a car bomb would make all this business more credible. And I'd feel better if you let us take up the surveillance you're running. In fact I'm going to have to insist."

"Then you'll want a make on a van license plate, and I've got the number of a certain motel room that'll bear watching," Cusick replied. "Got a pencil and pad handy?"

"We're professionals too," said Corwin. "Shoot."

By late afternoon, Bobby Lathrop began to feel tendrils of prickly heat on the nape of his neck. He'd tried several times to raise Pam Garza at her apartment and at work; had even tried Ramsay's number without success. With twenty-twenty hindsight, he knew he should've grabbed her the night before instead of howling off in that futile effort to nail Ramsay. Harman, who knew better than to go within two hundred yards of the Genie, had posted himself in the mall where he would hear the explosion. He had called twice to say the Genie was still intact, unobliterated. They had to presume Ramsay was still at work, maybe on a remote job, but sooner or later he'd come back for his toy. Bobby didn't want to call Unruh yet, but he knew that Unruh, at home on medical leave or some such, would be furious if that call didn't come. Bobby knew he should go to a pay phone to call, but then he might miss a call from Harman. He did it the easy way, with his scrambler, from the room.

Scrambler or no scrambler, Unruh didn't sound so hot. "No, of course he hasn't called here; he'd damned well better not, without a scrambler. Have you got the girl?"

"Which girl, Terence?"

"*Any* girl! Or Ramsay. Or any leads on any of them."

Bobby tried to explain, but sometimes there was no explaining failure. He assured Unruh that Ramsay would be accounted for almost any moment now, and that the Garza woman couldn't just disappear. He said he didn't know whether there was any fresh action at Jondahl's place.

"I called in a favor," Unruh replied, deliberately vague. "Sheriff's people have an open homicide there, forensics people borrowed from Gaithersburg. The place is blown, forget it. Unless you left prints there," he added ominously.

"Now you know I wouldn't be that dumb. And the Firebird's stored, beat to shit; we're using the van and a rented 'Vette. Listen, you have to figure that little kid is finding her way home. I could surveil her apartment, maybe pick her up if she didn't go to the nearest police cruiser. Unless you could put someone else on it," he added hopefully. "And what do I do with Garza, if I find her?"

"Hold incommunicado, either or both of them. I'll see if I can borrow some assets to find Garza; you can try the

Ramsay woman's apartment for the little girl, it's already got new tenants, but watch yourself. Somebody else could be around, God knows who. And Bobby: call me again the instant you have the news on Ramsay."

Bobby replaced the receiver thoughtfully, wondering if he was ever going to have good news on Ramsay.

Seventy yards away, in the closetlike telephone service module of the motel, a slender technician pressed a button, then another, then tapped out an instruction. His companion, older and burly, had given up on optimism years ago. "Too quick for you," he suggested to the young police tech.

"Nope. It was all scrambled mush, but whoever's on the other end has very high-tech stuff. And he responded from the rez of one," he consulted the readout, "Terence Unruh. Ever hear of him?"

"Naw. But I figure we're going to," said the burly one, "after I call this in to Corwin."

". . . And they're here," said the President's secretary, "and the phrase is Code Blue. General Magnuson said you'd understand. He seems very, ah, intent, Mr. President."

Harrison Rand leaned forward, flogging his memory. Codes yellow and red dealt with external threats; Code Blue had something to do with clear and present *internal* danger. "Well, I suppose it can't be helped. You'd better ring Walt, he's only across the street."

"For your ears only, sir. That's what they said, sir."

Rand sighed, threw up his hands, and handed a bundle of unsigned documents to his aide. "Give me one minute, and show them in," he said to the intercom. To the aide and the two men who stood near the big desk he said, "I'm afraid it'll have to wait, boys. Use that door," he added with a sweep of his hand. He stood up, pushing his glasses away from his nose as he dry-washed his face, wondering what in the name of the Lord God Almighty was so important that the Army's Magnuson had to bring Major General McManus of the Defense Intelligence Agency along for backup.

Magnuson entered with due respect, a rawboned gray eminence with piercing eyes, also gray; McManus stayed half a pace behind, shorter, not so gray but just as grim. They met the Presidential handclasp firmly, the DIA's McManus glancing around with something more than idle curiosity. "Now what's all this about Code Blue," Rand asked, smiling.

"Recordings," McManus muttered.

Magnuson: "Right. Mr. President, what I have to tell you is—well, a little bizarre. I don't think you want it taped. In fact, I think we should talk downstairs in the Situation Room because your own office, I'm horrified to say, may not be secure."

Rand nodded. "Anything you can tell me, you can tell Walter Kalvin. I'm calling him now," he said.

"Yessir," said McManus, before Magnuson could respond. "And you may want to call this person, too. With your permission, Mr. President," he finished, and scribbled a few words on the notepad in his hand.

Rand took the paper, saw the words, KALVIN IMPLICATED. ELECTRONICS WHIZ. He flushed, opened his mouth, then closed it again. "Maybe I can handle this alone," he said then, thrusting the note in his pocket. He strode into the hallway toward the stairs and nodded to another aide who crossed his path, but did not speak until they had been ushered into the map-lined Situation Room with its quiet whirr of communications equipment. Then: "How d'you know we're secure here?"

"Because DIA helps NSA sweep this room regularly, and Walter Kalvin has no clout here," said Magnuson, omitting the honorific. Then remembering it: "Mr. President, either we've been taken in by the hoax of the century, or—well, Metropolitan Police are backing the allegations up to a point. So far the casualties include Undersecretary Richard Parker; a fine old CIA alumnus named Wintoon; and a woman who just happened to get in the way. The score could climb at any time."

"General, do you have any idea how this sounds to me?" The President was smiling gently.

"Just like it sounded to me at fifteen hundred hours today, when I returned a call to a man I trust. Guess I'd better start this like a briefing," Magnuson said. He paused, setting his mental files in order, and then began. "Mr. President, do you ever watch Alan Ramsay on NBN?"

EIGHTEEN

By EIGHT O'CLOCK THE FOLLOWING MORNING, THE DESK top in Harrison Rand's Oval Office resembled a repairman's nightmare. One of the two men from No Such Agency—an insider's joke for the National Security Agency—began to remove heavy shielding from around a ceramic container the size of a man's hand. Electrical leads from the box were still connected to a maze of wiring that composed elements of the Presidential telephone system. "We can take it out of the system," he said. "Gamma signatures are negative for explosives."

Rand himself had been cautioned not to enter by McManus, both of them remaining a safe distance from the suspect device the NSA had found in the desk. Advised that the Oval Office was safe, the President strode in with stormclouds on his face, General McManus at his heels. "I think this is thin baloney, gentlemen. My closest friend would not endanger me," he said.

As the senior man lowered a screen-equipped device to

the carpet, McManus murmured, "Maybe not, Mr. President, but that box isn't a necessary element, and Kalvin is one of the few people with access to this room in your absence." Raising his voice: "Walton, what do you make of it?"

The senior man squinted down at the desk. "The thing has an antenna strip. That implies a short-range receiver and relay inside so someone nearby could activate its circuits, whatever they do. All we know now is, it may affect the telephone output, it's hermetically sealed, and it won't blow up."

Harrison Rand no longer trusted anyone entirely. He was not even certain that Walt Kalvin had done anything out of line. "How do you know it won't, if you haven't opened it," he said, stepping back a pace.

"Thermal neutron emitter," said McManus, as the junior man began to pull the leads from the ceramic box. "Explosives will return characteristic patterns of gamma rays."

The junior man supplied, "It's the sort of thing they're putting in airports these—Christ," he ended softly, raising his fingers to his mouth.

They could all hear faint cracklings from the box, and the polymer protector beneath it began to smoke. The junior man used diagonal cutters to sever the other wires as McManus wrestled a segment of shielding into place. The senior man used the cutters and a screwdriver as tongs, dropping the box onto the shielding, where it continued to sizzle for some time. "Energy cell," said the senior man, "one'll get you five. Fed from the bus bar and when power's removed it gives it all back to the internals. Nothing that'd look incriminating on X-ray or gamma return. We should've given it a portable power supply."

Rand approached the device. "Could you put that in English?"

"Yessir. Whoever installed that box knew enough electronics to avoid putting explosives in it. We'd find it in a sweep, which we do regularly. So he set it up to fry its circuits if anybody tried to disconnect it. Smart. That's what it did. Heated the whole box up, in fact.''

"Then you won't find anything inside?''

"Probably nothing useful, sir. The perpetrator was very determined that nobody else would learn just what that box did.''

"And he outsmarted you,'' said the President.

"I'm dreadfully sorry to say he did, sir. We were just in too big a hurry.''

That's how Walt would think, Rand reflected. Aloud he said, "Well, try and get everything put back so I can use my confounded office.'' He gestured for the general to follow and swept out, heading for the little think tank room. Then, behind closed doors: "McManus, I intend to find out just what that gizmo did. Any ideas?''

"Yes, sir, if you don't believe Ramsay. Let NSA check the cordless mike you use—and put Kalvin's butt on a griddle.''

"Walt keeps it himself. Always did; fanatic about it,'' Rand said thoughtfully.

"No doubt. And there's no telling how he's got *that* booby-trapped. Maybe his pal, Unruh, would know.''

"Oh; CIA, I believe.''

"Right; long and distinguished service, but he's a dying man. Metro Police say Terence Unruh may be running the men who tried to car-bomb Ramsay. And it's not exactly a long shot for Unruh to be hooked up with Kalvin. We're letting them run loose for the moment, looking for wider infection.''

Now the storm began to break, as the righteous Presidential anger of Harrison Rand began to surface. The Kalvin-Unruh connection, he knew, was a fact. "I still have a few groups to speak to on that media council thing, which is due for a vote soon. McManus, I want no action from you whatever, do you understand? None! Nor a whisper of any of this. I'll get that cordless mike myself, Walt will want me to use it anyhow."

"But Mr. President—"

"That's the end of it! It's a terrible thing to suspect you've gained the highest office in this country as someone's trained seal, honking on cue. I will be blast—no, I will be *damned* if I don't put an end to it myself."

McManus started to speak, hesitated, then pressed on: "Are you sure you want to know the answers?"

Sighing: "Absolutely. General, in many ways I'm the apotheosis of the common man. I'm not so stupid that I don't know I have limitations, and it has been my pride—which goeth before a fall—that my political career was not built on compromises with corruption. Not that I knew about." He remained silent for a moment. Then, "It was Warren Harding who said he could handle his enemies but his *friends* were ruining him. I won't be another Harding." He leaned over and activated the intercom. "Jeanette, buzz Walt Kalvin for me; remind him I—we—have a pep talk scheduled for those hardcore media liberals at two-fifteen. Oh, and Jeanette: that telephone maintenance never happened. It was a non-event." He toggled the intercom off. "I'm still not certain Walt has betrayed me, McManus. But I'll admit I'm seeing rat tracks everywhere."

Now even Harman was getting jumpy, and Bobby Lathrop had to admit the situation was out of control. No one was using Ramsay's apartment; the man had still not surfaced. Nor had the kid, or the Garza chick. Because they didn't want to risk butting heads with NBN security on its own turf, both men staked themselves out at the mall. Ramsay was a Name, and sooner or later he'd show up at the studios, probably by the back entrance where Bobby would see him.

It was beyond hope that Ramsay would come bouncing across the parking lot with a hot-looking number beside him; beyond dreaming that the chick would be Garza. But they must have been using Garza's red Honda. Bobby barely had time to use his comm set to bring Harman on the run, before he put himself on an intercept course on foot. As it happened, his path took him within a few feet of that damned Genie, which he hadn't looked under because he had too much sense to risk jouncing it even a little. Hot damn, nothing but dry holes for an eternity, and now two birds at once!

Bobby's coat was wide so it would hide the stubby little Ingram stuttergun. It was no trouble at all for him to move ahead of them near the back entrance, then turn as they approached, letting the muzzle protrude so that it showed but would be inconspicuous to distant shoppers. "No yelling or running, folks," he said as the two of them were even with the yellow Genie, and he saw Ramsay's gaze fixate on the Ingram. "Or I'll drop you right here."

The Garza hotsy stumbled when she recognized Bobby, saw him in all his commanding potency. "To think I used to follow your orders," she said.

Ramsay had one hand in a jacket pocket and Bobby nearly wasted him as the guy jerked his hands up to steady the woman. But the hands were empty. "You must be suicidal. We're being watched," was all he said.

"Nice try," Bobby said, seeing no one and feeling pretty good. "Now I want you to turn around and walk nice and steady out to my van."

The woman looked around, panicky, and Ramsay was pale too, but kept his head. "If I do, I'm dead," he said. And before Bobby could stop him, *he leaned on the Genie!*

Bobby almost fainted. "Get away from there!" he screamed, flinching, dropping the Ingram's muzzle, and that's when the Garza bimbo started slashing him with her nails.

Bobby hunched, the big shoulders flexing, and elbowed her in the boobs and nobody would have been fooled by that roundhouse right that Ramsay threw except that Bobby's attention was split, and he took only part of the blow on his pectorals, the rest of it rattling his china, and then the silly bastard was trying to wrestle the Ingram away from a man who could bench press the Washington Monument.

The woman started yodeling for help but she had both hands on Bobby's head, too, razoring across his eyes, and to shake her off he spun to the left and suddenly Ramsay's footwork got lucky, tangling Bobby's feet, and when they fell onto the hood of the car all Bobby could see was yellow, and in his mind, a gigantic black mushroom lifting them all into the sky. Bobby started yelling some himself at that point, trying to tell the crazy sonofabitch that little car was about to blow, but while his mouth was open Ramsay butted him even though Bobby still had a good grip on the Ingram and could have taken the older guy with one hand behind him only the Ingram burped, just three rounds but they all went past Bobby's cheek, and between trying to protect the trigger and flailing to get up off of the rocking, shuddering Genie, there wasn't much concentration left for martial arts.

Bobby took another head butt in the mouth, his personal chimes ringing like a carillon, and that's when he began to lose it, wondering when the fucking bomb would blow, sliding into blackness, letting go of the gun. At the edge of his awareness, he could hear big feet pounding near and voices that sounded anything but pleased. Then Bobby let go of everything.

When he came to, the first thing he saw was Harman, acting all surprised and innocent with his forty-five in the hands of a guy in plain clothes and with Harman himself in the hands of two other guys, and then somebody was reading them their Mirandas. "Don't shove the fucking car," Bobby managed to say as they hauled him to his feet. "Blow uth all to shit," he explained through broken incisors.

"I doubt it," said the balding plainclothesman. "Your little surprise was disarmed ten minutes after you put it there."

"Lithen, thith ith a mithtake, we're in intelligenthe too," Bobby said.

"You know what you're in," said the old guy. "You're in the dumper. And we're about to flush it."

Walter Kalvin strolled across the opening from the Executive Office Building to the West Wing shortly before two P.M. with the Donnersprache mike in an inside pocket and a set of unanswered questions beating in his skull. If Unruh didn't produce Ramsay or the kid by sundown, it would be time for some give and take with Harry Rand. Harry, devout do-gooder that he was, was still only a man, with a human failing where power was concerned. And whatever else Walt might have done, he could claim that he'd done it for Harry, and for the American people.

And if that didn't work, there was always that little fling Harry had taken with Pam Garza a decade before. Harry would give a lot to keep that out of the news, and even more to keep it from Bea Rand.

Before going to the Oval Office Kalvin detoured quickly down to the theatre, nodding to the security staff, taking a quick look through a viewport into the theatre. He had the list of attendees, but you never knew when Showers might lobby to have a couple of extras, and—

Kalvin blinked, denying the testimony of his eyes, while a flood of liquid helium poured through his veins. All the major networks were represented, which was merely irksome. The horrifying image was the sight of Alan Ramsay, looking as though he could hardly wait for Harry's little speech.

And why would Ramsay let himself be dragged within a mile of the White House, knowing what he knew? *Only if he had protection I don't know about,* Kalvin's pessimism replied.

Walter Kalvin turned on his heel and hurried up the stairs, not quite running. No one seemed to notice when he trotted from the West Wing back toward his own office, but he was breathless as he turned the corner in the hallway. In thirty seconds he could have the spare Donnersprache, the fake ID, and the money he kept in his wall safe.

His secretary was not on duty, and that alerted him. What electrified him were the men he saw as he eased a two-inch crack in the door to his inner office. Burly, clean-cut, in dark three piece suits, they were doing a careful toss of his office. Or rather, one was doing the toss, very quietly. The other stood before the wall safe, attending to a digital meter with leads to suction cups on the face of the safe. Probably FBI.

Kalvin took several steps backward in silence. As he reached the hallway he began to run.

Though Falls Church adjoins Arlington, it retains its own frumpy character. Kalvin left the Greyhound local and then watched the sun disappear beyond the old rooftops along Broad Street, expecting the car from the east, toward Arlington, because that was where Unruh lived. Kalvin had lost his touch with this kind of skulking in thirty years, and did not recognize the blue Caddie until it nearly ran him down.

Terry Unruh had been a good-looking specimen only a few months before. Late shadows accentuated the ravages to the flesh of his face. Unruh's was a death's head, almost bald, with a gray pallor. "My wife tried to stop me," said Unruh as the Caddie bore them toward a pink sunset. "She outweighs me, now."

Kalvin was in no mood to make small talk, and changed the subject. "They'll be watching every major airport, but of course you'd know that," he said.

The death's head nodded. "Leesburg Municipal is not a major airport," it said. "You have the full exfiltration kit? Enough cash?"

"Enough." *But I couldn't take the risk of hitting my safe deposit boxes. I did transfer a small fortune from one offshore bank to another; both Brit. I wonder what you'd do if you knew that Bermuda account of yours was gutted now. You might suspect that if you knew I was low on cash.*

Unruh drove expertly for a dead man. He overtook a limo, probably headed for Dulles, and settled back into the traffic stream. "We'll have to wait 'til dark. After that it's only a two hour hop to Canada," he said.

Kalvin made no reply, keeping his frustrations in check because Unruh was his lifeline. A few miles farther, Unruh snapped on his lights. "You know, I never did have a clear picture what you were up to, Kalvin."

"You'll hear enough about it, I'm sure."

"Oh, I already have, right after I got your mayday this afternoon. Mid-level spook, friend of mine. He didn't dream I might be connected with you; must be kicking himself by now." A long silence ensued. Unruh broke it himself. "I had the idea that this was just some little political edge of yours, nothing that'd change things much, no worse than the nits you find in any administration. Imagine my surprise," he added with rich sarcasm.

"I'd rather not discuss it," Kalvin said, as Unruh swung the Caddie off of the Leesburg Pike.

"Why not? You must be the most convincing discusser since Moses heard from the burning bush. Why didn't you use that charisma machine yourself?"

"It helps to have the right voice to begin with," Kalvin said grudgingly. "And the right background."

"Like being born with U.S. citizenship? That occurred

to me this afternoon." Now Unruh turned off the paved county road onto a rutted farm access path. To their right, no more than a few miles distant, an airport beacon flashed its brief surge of welcome. The Caddie slowed, then stopped.

"Don't tell me," said Kalvin, keeping his tone steady despite a thrill of alarm.

"No, *you* tell *me*," said Unruh, sounding very tired. "Use your powers of electronic persuasion. Or won't it work without a boxful of equipment?"

"Start the fucking car, Terry," said Kalvin; and when Unruh did not move, he drew the Donnersprache mike from his coat. "Here it is. Is this your price for getting me exfiltrated? Take it," he said. *With the microfilmed diagrams in my billfold, I can build more when I get to Argentina.*

As Terence Unruh took the cordless mike, like a cold sceptre signaling the transfer of power, he laughed briefly. It became a cough, and required all of Unruh's strength to control. "You've already paid my price," he said, and drew a stubby little automatic with his left hand. "But there's a price for freedom; everybody's, I mean. They always told me that price was eternal vigilance. Sounds terribly mundane, doesn't it?"

Walter Kalvin said nothing, waiting for Unruh to pick up the dialogue; to lead him to some further compromise. The last, and most horrifying, surprise of his life was the simultaneous sound and shock of a short nine-millimeter round entering his left side.

"No messy trials for us, Kalvin," said Unruh.

Because the little weapon had only modest impact, Kalvin was able to turn, grappling for the pistol, though he already felt something hideously wrong with his lungs. The second and third rounds seemed not quite so loud, their impacts less astounding. "No! Enough," he said, and oddly enough, Unruh did not fire again. Through a vast sense of disappointment, and shock that had somehow not entirely converted to pain, Kalvin realized that he was going to die more in curiosity than in agony. "You expect to use it yourself?"

Only the instrument cluster lit the face of Terence Unruh, a corpse face in faint green reflection. "No. This is more important than money to my children. I'm turning it in."

Now Kalvin felt himself sliding sideways and fumbled in his pocket with his right hand for the microphone's remote controller. "No you won't," he said, now with a sense of fullness as internal bleeding took its course. He could no longer see Unruh, but he could feel the device in his pocket.

The cordless microphone contained only fifty grams of explosive, not enough to completely demolish the car. But the concussion wave and flying particles were enough to eliminate all pain and disappointment from both men forever.

NINETEEN

". . . AND SO IT SEEMS THAT WE LIVE BY CATCH phrases," said Alan Ramsay, beginning his windup of 'The Ramsay File' before eighty million Americans. In less than forty-eight hours, the Donnersprache unit from Kalvin's wall safe had been disarmed and analyzed. Ramsay leaned against a display table as he spoke, sometimes using the cordless mike to demonstrate it, while the pointers of delicate meters responded to enhanced elements of resonance and pitch. "But we can be destroyed by catch phrases, too, when they happen to be the wrong ones, made artificially attractive."

He raised the microphone again. "Violence never settled anything," he intoned, glancing at the meters, adding, "and if you believe that, you never saw a war, a catfight, or a football game." Now he smiled faintly. "You can't cheat an honest man. Democracy means that all opinions are equal. And finally, cheaters never win." He lowered the mike, looking at it as though it were something to scrape off his shoe. "Well, in this case the cheater finally lost; but we'd be well advised not to count on it.

"And what's to be done with this little device, now that our Chief Executive has denounced its use? That isn't my decision, of course. But it seems that we have several options: make it available from Radio Shack for twenty-nine ninety-five, perhaps. Outlaw it as we did anabolic steroids and subliminal advertising? Maybe. Our chief defense springs from the same technology that created it; now that we can spot it, we'll know when it's being used against us.

"Because it *is* a weapon against us, against the kind of critical thinking that separates truth from lies. Nazi Germany had a leader who used Donnersprache with deliberate savagery. The measure of Harrison Rand is that, even though the device—arguably—put him in the White House, he reacted with courage, and outrage, when he discovered it. In the game of politics, where power is the name of the game, how could we ask for more?

"From Washington, this is Alan Ramsay for NBN."

As the monitor light winked out, Ramsay turned to retrieve the central exhibit, handing it to one of the team detailed to secure it. Grinning, the man said, "Radio Shack! Don't hold your breath."

"Avoid giving long odds," Ramsay said. "Your grandfather could've bought a kingdom for a radar detector."

Irv, his headset awry, gripped Ramsay's arm with both hands in jubilation. "Knockout, Alan, just bleeding dynamite! If this didn't outdraw the Super Bowl, I'll buy dinner."

"I'll take a raincheck; got a date with two gorgeous creatures," Ramsay cracked, pulling off his tie, hurrying toward a floorman who offered the usual towel so that he could begin ridding himself of makeup.

Minutes later, face scrubbed, Ramsay found Laurie waiting with Pam Garza. Laurie seemed undecided whether to shake his hand or leap into his arms and compromised by hugging him around the midriff. "You were great, Dad," she beamed.

Pam gave him a chaste kiss and fell in step with the Ramsays. "You showed a lot of restraint," she said. "If I hadn't listened carefully I wouldn't have known you had any personal involvement."

"Modest heroism is my forte," he said, deadpan, then winked. "Anyway, I already knew I'm scheduled for the cover of *Newsweek*." Laurie squealed and applauded. "I passed over Tom Cusick's group, too; their idea, actually. Publicity wouldn't do them any good. Unruh's family, either. From that note he left, he must've known he wasn't coming back. There's poetic justice for you; some people I loved aren't coming back either because of him."

"Hey, you haven't mentioned our new outfits," Pam said, trying to divert his train of thought, preening in her finery. "You said 'just short of formal,' but you didn't say which McDonald's you had in mind."

"Smartass," Ramsay replied. "Let's just say someone else is picking up the tab for the limo."

"Limo? Wow, Dad," Laurie marveled. "You've gotta tell us where."

"Well, uh—believe it or not, the White House, pudd'n."

Pam hesitated. "Me, too? Alan, you know why I can't—much as I'd love to."

"Sure you can," he said. "All that stuff happened a long time ago, to two different people. Just look him in the eye, but curtsy while you do it."

"My God," she said, and then giggled. "He's probably after your vote."

Trotting down the stairs toward the front entrance, Ramsay laughed aloud. "That'll be the day; our retreaded preacher is a lousy judge of character. But I have an idea he'd be a great companion on a hunting trip.''

He leaned forward to open a door and stumbled, laughing at himself, as it was opened for him. Outside, the limo waited.

UNIVERSE
by Robert A. Heinlein

The Proxima Centauri Expedition, sponsored by the Jordan Foundation in 2119, was the first recorded attempt to reach the nearer stars of this galaxy. Whatever its unhappy fate we can only conjecture. . . .

—Quoted from *The Romance of Modern Astrography*, by Franklin Buck, published by Lux Transcriptions, Ltd., 3.50 cr.

"THERE'S A MUTIE! LOOK OUT!"

At the shouted warning, Hugh Hoyland ducked, with nothing to spare. An egg-sized iron missile clanged against the bulkhead just above his scalp with force that promised a fractured skull. The speed with which he crouched had lifted his feet from the floor plates. Before his body could settle slowly to the deck, he planted his feet against the bulkhead behind him and shoved. He went shooting down the passageway in a long, flat dive, his knife drawn and ready.

He twisted in the air, checked himself with his feet against the opposite bulkhead at the turn in the passage from which the mutie had attacked him, and floated lightly to his feet. The other branch of the passage was empty. His two companions joined him, sliding awkwardly across the floor plates.

"Is it gone?" demanded Alan Mahoney.

"Yes," agreed Hoyland. "I caught a glimpse of it as it ducked down that hatch. A female, I think. Looked like it had four legs."

"Two legs or four, we'll never catch it now," commented the third man.

"Who the Huff wants to catch it?" protested Mahoney. "*I* don't."

"Well, I do, for one," said Hoyland. "By Jordan, if its aim had been two inches better, I'd be ready for the Converter."

"Can't either one of you two speak three words without swearing?" the third man disapproved. "What if the Captain could hear you?" He touched his forehead reverently as he mentioned the Captain.

"Oh, for Jordan's sake," snapped Hoyland, "don't be so stuffy, Mort Tyler. You're not a scientist yet. I reckon I'm as devout as you are—there's no grave sin in occasionally giving vent to your feelings. Even the scientists do it. I've heard 'em."

Tyler opened his mouth as if to expostulate, then apparently thought better of it.

Mahoney touched Hoyland on the arm. "Look, Hugh," he pleaded, "let's get out of here. We've never been this high before. I'm jumpy—I want to get back down to where I can feel some weight on my feet."

Hoyland looked longingly toward the hatch through which his assailant had disappeared while his hand rested on the grip of his knife, then he turned to Mahoney. "O.K., kid," he agreed, "it's a long trip down anyhow."

He turned and slithered back toward the hatch, whereby they had reached the level where they now were, the other two following him. Disregarding the ladder by which they had mounted, he stepped off into the opening and floated slowly down to the deck fifteen feet below, Tyler and Mahoney close behind him. Another hatch, staggered a few feet from the first, gave access to a still lower deck. Down, down, down, and still farther down they dropped, tens and dozens of decks, each silent, dimly lighted, mysterious. Each time they fell a little faster, landed a little harder. Mahoney protested at last.

"Let's walk the rest of the way, Hugh. That last jump hurt my feet."

"All right. But it will take longer. How far have we got to go? Anybody keep count?"

"We've got about seventy decks to go to reach farm country," answered Tyler.

"How do you know?" demanded Mahoney suspiciously.

"I counted them, stupid. And as we came down I took one away for each deck."

"You did not. Nobody but a scientist can do numbering like that. Just because you're learning to read and write you think you know everything."

Hoyland cut in before it could develop into a quarrel. "Shut up, Alan. Maybe he can do it. He's clever about such things. Anyhow, it feels like about seventy decks—I'm heavy enough."

"Maybe he'd like to count the blades on my knife."

"Stow it, I said. Dueling is forbidden outside the village. That is the Rule." They proceeded in silence, running lightly down the stairways until increasing weight on each succeeding level forced them to a more pedestrian pace. Presently they broke through into a level that was

quite brilliantly lighted and more than twice as deep between decks as the ones above it. The air was moist and
warm; vegetation obscured the view.

"Well, down at last," said Hugh. "I don't recognize
this farm; we must have come down by a different line
than we went up."

"There's a farmer," said Tyler. He put his little fingers
to his lips and whistled, then called, "Hey! Shipmate!
Where are we?"

The peasant looked them over slowly, then directed them
in reluctant monosyllables to the main passageway which
would lead them back to their own village.

A brisk walk of a mile and a half down a wide tunnel
moderately crowded with traffic—travelers, porters, an occasional pushcart, a dignified scientist swinging in a litter
borne by four husky orderlies and preceded by his master-
at-arms to clear the common crew out of the way—a mile
and a half of this brought them to the common of their
own village, a spacious compartment three decks high and
perhaps ten times as wide. They split up and went their
own ways, Hugh to his quarters in the barracks of the
cadets—young bachelors who did not live with their parents. He washed himself, and went thence to the compartments of his uncle, for whom he worked for his meals.
His aunt glanced up as he came in, but said nothing, as
became a woman.

His uncle said, "Hello, Hugh. Been exploring again?"

"Good eating, Uncle. Yes."

His uncle, a stolid, sensible man, looked tolerantly
amused. "Where did you go and what did you find?"

Hugh's aunt had slipped silently out of the compartment, and now returned with his supper which she placed
before him. He fell to—it did not occur to him to thank
her. He munched a bite before replying.

"Up. We climbed almost to the level-of-no-weight. A
mutie tried to crack my skull."

His uncle chuckled. "You'll find your death in those passageways, lad. Better you should pay more attention to my business against the day when I'll die and get out of your way."

Hugh looked stubborn. "Don't you have any curiosity, Uncle?"

"Me? Oh, I was prying enough when I was a lad. I followed the main passage all the way around and back to the village. Right through the Dark Sector I went, with muties tagging my heels. See that scar?"

Hugh glanced at it perfunctorily. He had seen it many times before and heard the story repeated to boredom. Once around the Ship—*pfui!* He wanted to go everywhere, see everything, and find out the why of things. Those upper levels now—if men were not intended to climb that high, why had Jordan created them?

But he kept his own counsel and went on with his meal. His uncle changed the subject. "I've occasion to visit the Witness. John Black claims I owe him three swine. Want to come along?"

"Why, no, I guess not—Wait—I believe I will."

"Hurry up, then."

They stopped at the cadets' barracks, Hugh claiming an errand. The Witness lived in a small, smelly compartment directly across the Common from the barracks, where he would be readily accessible to any who had need of his talents. They found him sitting in his doorway, picking his teeth with a fingernail. His apprentice, a pimply-faced adolescent with an intent nearsighted expression, squatted behind him.

"Good eating," said Hugh's uncle.

"Good eating to you, Edard Hoyland. D'you come on business, or to keep an old man company?"

"Both," Hugh's uncle returned diplomatically, then explained his errand.

"So?" said the Witness. "Well—the contract's clear enough:

> "Black John delivered ten bushels of oats,
> Expecting his pay in a pair of shoats;
> Ed brought his sow to breed for pig;
> John gets his pay when the pigs grow big.

"How big are the pigs now, Edard Hoyland?"

"Big enough," acknowledged Hugh's uncle, "but Black claims three instead of two."

"Tell him to go soak his head. 'The Witness has spoken.' "

He laughed in a thin, high cackle.

The two gossiped for a few minutes, Edard Hoyland digging into his recent experiences to satisfy the old man's insatiable liking for details. Hugh kept decently silent while the older men talked. But when his uncle turned to go he spoke up. "I'll stay awhile, Uncle."

"Eh? Suit yourself. Good eating, Witness."

"Good eating, Edard Hoyland."

"I've brought you a present, Witness," said Hugh, when his uncle had passed out of hearing.

"Let me see it."

Hugh produced a package of tobacco which he had picked up from his locker at the barracks. The Witness accepted it without acknowledgment, then tossed it to his apprentice, who took charge of it.

"Come inside," invited the Witness, then directed his speech to his apprentice. "Here, you—fetch the cadet a chair."

"Now, lad," he added as they sat themselves down, "tell me what you have been doing with yourself."

Hugh told him, and was required to repeat in detail all the incidents of his more recent explorations, the Witness complaining the meanwhile over his inability to remember exactly everything he saw.

"You youngsters have no capacity," he pronounced. "No capacity. Even that lout"—he jerked his head toward the apprentice—"he has none, though he's a dozen times better than you. Would you believe it, he can't soak up a thousand lines a day, yet he expects to sit in my seat when I am gone. Why, when I was apprenticed, I used to sing myself to sleep on a mere thousand lines. Leaky vessels—that's what you are."

Hugh did not dispute the charge, but waited for the old man to go on, which he did in his own time.

"You had a question to put to me, lad?"

"In a way, Witness."

"Well—out with it. Don't chew your tongue."

"Did you ever climb all the way up to no-weight?"

"Me? Of course not. I was a Witness, learning my calling. I had the lines of all the Witnesses before me to learn, and no time for boyish amusements."

"I had hoped you could tell me what I would find there."

"Well, now, that's another matter. I've never climbed, but I hold the memories of more climbers than you will ever see. I'm an old man. I knew your father's father, and his grandsire before that. What is it you want to know?"

"Well—" What was it he wanted to know? How could he ask a question that was no more than a gnawing ache in his breast? Still—"What is it all for, Witness? Why are there all those levels above us?"

"Eh? How's that? Jordan's name, son—I'm a Witness, not a scientist."

"Well—I thought you must know. I'm sorry."

"But I do know. What you want is the Lines from the Beginning."

"I've heard them."

"Hear them again. All your answers are in there, if

you've the wisdom to see them. Attend me. No—this is a chance for my apprentice to show off his learning. Here, you! The Lines from the Beginning—and mind your rhythm.''

The apprentice wet his lips with his tongue and began:
''In the Beginning there was Jordan, thinking His lonely thoughts alone.

In the Beginning there was darkness, formless, dead, and Man unknown.

Out of the loneness came a longing, out of the longing came a vision,

Out of the dream there came a planning, out of the plan there came decision—

Jordan's hand was lifted and the Ship was born!

Mile after mile of snug compartments, tank by tank for the golden corn,

Ladder and passage, door and locker, fit for the needs of the yet unborn.

He looked on His work and found it pleasing, meet for a race that was yet to be.

He thought of Man—Man came into being—checked his thought and searched for the key.

Man untamed would shame his Maker, Man unruled would spoil the Plan;

So Jordan made the Regulations, orders to each single man,

Each to a task and each to a station, serving a purpose beyond their ken,

Some to speak and some to listen—order came to the ranks of men.

Crew He created to work at their stations, scientists to guide the Plan.

Over them all He created the Captain, made him judge of the race of Man.

Thus it was in the Golden Age!

Jordan is perfect, all below him lack perfection in their
    deeds.
Envy, Greed, and Pride of Spirit sought for minds to lodge
    their seeds.
One there was who gave them lodging—accursed Huff, the
    first to sin!
His evil counsel stirred rebellion, planted doubt where it
    had not been;
Blood of martyrs stained the floor plates, Jordan's Captain
    made the Trip.
Darkness swallowed up—''

The old man gave the boy the back of his hand, sharp
across the mouth. "Try again!"
    "From the beginning?"
    "No! From where you missed."
    The boy hesitated, then caught his stride:

    "Darkness swallowed ways of virtue, Sin prevailed
    throughout the Ship. . . .''

The boy's voice droned on, stanza after stanza, reciting
at great length but with little sharpness of detail the old,
old story of sin, rebellion, and the time of darkness. How
wisdom prevailed at last and the bodies of the rebel lead-
ers were fed to the Converter. How some of the rebels
escaped making the Trip and lived to father the muties.
How a new Captain was chosen, after prayer and sacrifice.
    Hugh stirred uneasily, shuffling his feet. No doubt the
answers to his questions were there, since these were the
Sacred Lines, but he had not the wit to understand them.
Why? What was it all about? Was there really nothing
more to life than eating and sleeping and finally the long
Trip? Didn't Jordan intend for him to understand? Then
why this ache in his breast? This hunger that persisted in
spite of good eating?

While he was breaking his fast after sleep an orderly came to the door of his uncle's compartments. "The scientist requires the presence of Hugh Hoyland," he recited glibly.

Hugh knew that the scientist referred to was Lieutenant Nelson, in charge of the spiritual and physical welfare of the Ship's sector which included Hugh's native village. He bolted the last of his breakfast and hurried after the messenger.

"Cadet Hoyland!" he was announced. The scientist looked up from his own meal and said:

"Oh, yes. Come in, my boy. Sit down. Have you eaten?"

Hugh acknowledged that he had, but his eyes rested with interest on the fancy fruit in front of his superior. Nelson followed his glance. "Try some of these figs. They're a new mutation—I had them brought all the way from the far side. Go ahead—a man your age always has somewhere to stow a few more bites."

Hugh accepted with much self-consciousness. Never before had he eaten in the presence of a scientist. The elder leaned back in his chair, wiped his fingers on his shirt, arranged his beard, and started in.

"I haven't seen you lately, son. Tell me what you have been doing with yourself." Before Hugh could reply he went on: "No, don't tell me—I will tell you. For one thing you have been exploring, climbing, without too much respect for the forbidden areas. Is it not so?" He held the young man's eye. Hugh fumbled for a reply.

But he was let off again. "Never mind. I know, and you know that I know. I am not too displeased. But it has brought it forcibly to my attention that it is time that you decided what you are to do with your life. Have you any plans?"

"Well—no definite ones, sir."

"How about that girl, Edris Baxter? D'you intend to marry her?"

"Why—uh—I don't know, sir. I guess I want to, and her father is willing, I think. Only—"

"Only what?"

"Well—he wants me to apprentice to his farm. I suppose it's a good idea. His farm together with my uncle's business would make a good property."

"But you're not sure?"

"Well—I don't know."

"Correct. You're not for that. I have other plans. Tell me, have you ever wondered why I taught you to read and write? Of course, you have. But you've kept your own counsel. That is good.

"Now attend me. I've watched you since you were a small child. You have more imagination than the common run, more curiosity, more go. And you are a born leader. You were different even as a baby. Your head was too large, for one thing, and there were some who voted at your birth inspection to put you at once into the Converter. But I held them off. I wanted to see how you would turn out.

"A peasant life is not for the likes of you. You are to be a scientist."

The old man paused and studied his face. Hugh was confused, speechless. Nelson went on: "Oh, yes. Yes, indeed. For a man of your temperament, there are only two things to do with him: Make him one of the custodians, or send him to the Converter."

"Do you mean, sir, that I have nothing to say about it?"

"If you want to put it that bluntly—yes. To leave the bright ones among the ranks of the Crew is to breed heresy. We can't have that. We had it once and it almost destroyed the human race. You have marked yourself out by your exceptional ability; you must now be instructed in right thinking, be initiated into the mysteries, in order that you may be a conserving force rather than a focus of infection and a source of trouble.''

The orderly reappeared loaded down with bundles which he dumped on the deck. Hugh glanced at them, then burst out, ''Why, those are my things!''

''Certainly,'' acknowledged Nelson. ''I sent for them. You're to sleep here henceforth. I'll see you later and start you on your studies—unless you have something more on your mind?''

''Why, no, sir. I guess not. I must admit I am a little confused. I suppose—I suppose this means you don't want me to marry?''

''Oh, *that*,'' Nelson answered indifferently. ''Take her if you like—her father can't protest now. But let me warn you you'll grow tired of her.''

Hugh Hoyland devoured the ancient books that his mentor permitted him to read, and felt no desire for many, many sleeps to go climbing, or even to stir out of Nelson's cabin. More than once he felt that he was on the track of the secret—a secret as yet undefined, even as a question— but again he would find himself more confused than ever. It was evidently harder to reach the wisdom of scientisthood than he had thought.

Once, while he was worrying away at the curious twisted characters of the ancients and trying to puzzle out their odd rhetoric and unfamiliar terms, Nelson came into the little compartment that had been set aside for him, and, laying a fatherly hand on his shoulder, asked, ''How goes it, boy?''

''Why, well enough, sir, I suppose,'' he answered, laying the book aside. ''Some of it is not quite clear to me— not clear at all, to tell the truth.''

''That is to be expected,'' the old man said equably. ''I've let you struggle along by yourself at first in order that you may see the traps that native wit alone will fall into. Many of these things are not to be understood without instruction. What have you there?'' He picked up the book and glanced at it. It was inscribed *Basic Modern Physics*. ''So? This is one of the most valuable of the sacred writings, yet the uninitiate could not possibly make good use of it without help. The first thing that you must understand, my boy, is that our forefathers, for all their spiritual perfection, did not look at things in the fashion in which we do.

''They were incurable romantics, rather than rationalists, as we are, and the truths which they handed down to us, though strictly true, were frequently clothed in allegorical language. For example, have you come to the Law of Gravitation?''

''I read about it.''

''Did you understand it? No, I can see that you didn't.''

''Well,'' said Hugh defensively, ''it didn't seem to *mean* anything. It just sounded silly, if you will pardon me, sir.''

''That illustrates my point. You were thinking of it in literal terms, like the laws governing electrical devices found elsewhere in this same book. 'Two bodies attract each other directly as the product of their masses and inversely as the square of their distance.' It sounds like a rule for simple physical facts, does it not? Yet it is nothing of the sort; it was the poetical way the old ones had of expressing the rule of propinquity which governs the emotion of love. The bodies referred to are human bodies, mass is their capacity for love. Young people have a greater capacity for love than the elderly; when they are thrown together, they fall in love, yet when they are separated they soon get over it. 'Out of sight, out of mind.' It's as simple as that. But you were seeking some deep meaning for it.''

Hugh grinned. ''I never thought of looking at it that way. I can see that I am going to need a lot of help.''

''Is there anything else bothering you just now?''

"Well, yes, lots of things, though I probably can't remember them offhand. I mind one thing: Tell me, Father, can muties be considered as being people?"

"I can see you have been listening to idle talk. The answer to that is both yes and no. It is true that the muties originally descended from people but they are no longer part of the Crew—they cannot now be considered as members of the human race, for they have flouted Jordan's Law.

"This is a broad subject," he went on, settling down to it. "There is even some question as to the original meaning of the word 'mutie.' Certainly they number among their ancestors the mutineers who escaped death at the time of the rebellion. But they also have in their blood the blood of many of the mutants who were born during the dark age. You understand, of course, that during that period our present wise rule of inspecting each infant for the mark of sin and returning to the Converter any who are found to be mutations was not in force. There are strange and horrible things crawling through the dark passageways and lurking in the deserted levels."

Hugh thought about it for a while, then asked, "Why is it that mutations still show up among us, the people?"

"That is simple. The seed of sin is still in us. From time to time it still shows up, incarnate. In destroying those monsters we help to cleanse the stock and thereby bring closer the culmination of Jordan's Plan, the end of the Trip at our heavenly home, Far Centaurus."

Hoyland's brow wrinkled again. "That is another thing that I don't understand. Many of these ancient writings speak of the Trip as if it were an actual *moving*, a going-somewhere—as if the Ship itself were no more than a pushcart. How can that be?"

Nelson chuckled. "How can it, indeed? How can that move which is the background against which all else moves? The answer, of course, is plain. You have again mistaken allegorical language for the ordinary usage of everyday speech. Of course, the Ship is solid, immovable, in a physical sense. How can the whole universe move? Yet, it *does* move, in a spiritual sense. With every righteous act we move closer to the sublime destination of Jordan's Plan.''

Hugh nodded. ''I think I see.''

''Of course, it is conceivable that Jordan could have fashioned the world in some other shape than the Ship, had it suited His purpose. When man was younger and more poetical, holy men vied with one another in inventing fanciful worlds which Jordan might have created. One school invented an entire mythology of a topsy-turvy world of endless reaches of space, empty save for pinpoints of light and bodiless mythological monsters. They called it the heavenly world, or heaven, as if to contrast it with the solid reality of the Ship. They seemed never to tire of speculating about it, inventing details for it, and of making pictures of what they conceived it to be like. I suppose they did it to the greater glory of Jordan, and who is to say that He found their dreams unacceptable? But in this modern age we have more serious work to do.''

Hugh was not interested in astronomy. Even his untutored mind had been able to see in its wild extravagance an intention not literal. He turned to problems nearer at hand.

''Since the muties are the seed of sin, why do we make no effort to wipe them out? Would not that be an act that would speed the Plan?''

The old man considered a while before replying. ''That is a fair question and deserves a straight answer. Since you are to be a scientist you will need to know the answer. Look at it this way: There is a definite limit to the number of Crew the Ship can support. If our numbers increase without limit, there comes a time when there will not be good eating for all of us. Is it not better that some should die in brushes with the muties than that we should grow in numbers until we killed each other for food?

"The ways of Jordan are inscrutable. Even the muties have a part in His Plan."

It seemed reasonable, but Hugh was not sure.

But when Hugh was transferred to active work as a junior scientist in the operation of the Ship's functions, he found there were other opinions. As was customary, he put in a period serving the Converter. The work was not onerous; he had principally to check in the waste materials brought in by porters from each of the villages, keep books of their contributions, and make sure that no reclaimable metal was introduced into the first-stage hopper. But it brought him into contact with Bill Ertz, the Assistant Chief Engineer, a man not much older than himself.

He discussed with him the things he had learned from Nelson, and was shocked at Ertz's attitude.

"Get this through your head, kid," Ertz told him. "This is a practical job for practical men. Forget all that romantic nonsense. Jordan's Plan! That stuff is all right to keep the peasants quiet and in their place, but don't fall for it yourself. There is no Plan—other than our own plans for looking out for ourselves. The Ship has to have light and heat and power for cooking and irrigation. The Crew can't get along without those things and that makes us boss of the Crew.

"As for this softheaded tolerance toward the muties, you're going to see some changes made! Keep your mouth shut and string along with us."

It impressed on him that he was expected to maintain a primary loyalty to the bloc of younger men among the scientists. They were a well-knit organization within an organization and were made up of practical, hardheaded men who were working toward improvement of conditions throughout the Ship, as they saw them. They were well-knit because an apprentice who failed to see things their way did not last long. Either he failed to measure up and soon found himself back in the ranks of the peasants, or, as was more likely, suffered some mishap and wound up in the Converter.

And Hoyland began to see that they were right.

They were realists. The Ship was the Ship. It was a fact, requiring no explanation. As for Jordan—who had ever seen Him, spoken to Him? What was this nebulous Plan of His? The object of life was living. A man was born, lived his life, and then went to the Converter. It was as simple as that, no mystery to it, no sublime Trip and no Centaurus. These romantic stories were simply hangovers from the childhood of the race before men gained the understanding and the courage to look facts in the face.

He ceased bothering his head about astronomy and mystical physics and all the other mass of mythology he had been taught to revere. He was still amused, more or less, by the Lines from the Beginning and by all the old stories about Earth—what the Huff was "Earth," anyhow?—but now realized that such things could be taken seriously only by children and dullards.

Besides, there was work to do. The younger men, while still maintaining the nominal authority of their elders, had plans of their own, the first of which was a systematic extermination of the muties. Beyond that, their intentions were still fluid, but they contemplated making full use of the resources of the Ship, including the upper levels. The young men were able to move ahead with their plans without an open breach with their elders because the older scientists simply did not bother to any great extent with the routine of the Ship. The present Captain had grown so fat that he rarely stirred from his cabin; his aide, one of the young men's bloc, attended to affairs for him.

Hoyland never laid eyes on the Chief Engineer save once, when he showed up for the purely religious ceremony of manning landing stations.

The project of cleaning out the muties required reconnaissance of the upper levels to be done systematically. It was in carrying out such scouting that Hugh Hoyland was again ambushed by a mutie.

This mutie was more accurate with his slingshot. Hoyland's companions, forced to retreat by superior numbers, left him for dead.

Joe-Jim Gregory was playing himself a game of checkers. Time was when they had played cards together, but Joe, the head on the right, had suspected Jim, the left-hand member of the team, of cheating. They had quarreled about it, then given it up, for they both learned early in their joint career that two heads on one pair of shoulders must necessarily find ways of getting along together.

Checkers was better. They could both see the board, and disagreement was impossible.

A loud metallic knocking at the door of the compartment interrupted the game. Joe-Jim unsheathed his throwing knife and cradled it, ready for quick use. "Come in!" roared Jim.

The door opened, the one who had knocked backed into the room—the only safe way, as everyone knew, to enter Joe-Jim's presence. The newcomer was squat and ruggedly powerful, not over four feet in height. The relaxed body of a man hung across one shoulder and was steadied by a hand.

Joe-Jim returned the knife to its sheath. "Put it down, Bobo," Jim ordered.

"And close the door," added Joe. "Now what have we got here?"

It was a young man, apparently dead, though no wound appeared on him. Bobo patted a thigh. "Eat 'im?" he said hopefully. Saliva spilled out of his still-opened lips.

"Maybe," temporized Jim. "Did you kill him?"

Bobo shook his undersized head.

"Good Bobo," Joe approved. "Where did you hit him?"

"Bobo hit him *there*." The microcephalic shoved a broad thumb against the supine figure in the area between the umbilicus and the breastbone.

"Good shot," Joe approved. "We couldn't have done better with a knife."

"Bobo *good* shot," the dwarf agreed blandly. "Want see?" He twitched his slingshot invitingly.

"Shut up," answered Joe, not unkindly. "No, we don't want to see; we want to make him talk."

"Bobo fix," the short one agreed, and started with simple brutality to carry out his purpose.

Joe-Jim slapped him away, and applied other methods, painful but considerably less drastic than those of the dwarf. The younger man jerked and opened his eyes.

"Eat 'im?" repeated Bobo.

"No," said Joe. "When did you eat last?" inquired Jim.

Bobo shook his head and rubbed his stomach, indicating with graphic pantomime that it had been a long time—too long. Joe-Jim went over to a locker, opened it, and withdrew a haunch of meat. He held it up. Jim smelled it and Joe drew his head away in nose-wrinkling disgust. Joe-Jim threw it to Bobo, who snatched it happily out of the air. "Now, get out," ordered Jim.

Bobo trotted away, closing the door behind him. Joe-Jim turned to the captive and prodded him with his foot. "Speak up," said Jim. "Who the Huff are you?"

The young man shivered, put a hand to his head, then seemed suddenly to bring his surroundings into focus, for he scrambled to his feet, moving awkwardly against the low weight conditions of this level, and reached for his knife.

It was not at his belt.

Joe-Jim had his own out and brandished it. "Be good and you won't get hurt. What do they call you?"

The young man wet his lips, and his eyes hurried about the room. "Speak up," said Joe.

"Why bother with him?" inquired Jim. "I'd say he was only good for meat. Better call Bobo back."

"No hurry about that," Joe answered. "I want to talk to him. What's your name?"

The prisoner looked again at the knife and muttered, "Hugh Hoyland."

"That doesn't tell us much," Jim commented. "What d'you do? What village do you come from? And what were you doing in mutie country?"

But this time Hoyland was sullen. Even the prick of the knife against his ribs caused him only to bite his lips. "Shucks," said Joe, "he's only a stupid peasant. Let's drop it."

"Shall we finish him off?"

"No. Not now. Shut him up."

Joe-Jim opened the door of a small side compartment, and urged Hugh in with the knife. He then closed and fastened the door and went back to his game. "Your move, Jim."

The compartment in which Hugh was locked was dark. He soon satisfied himself by touch that the smooth steel walls were entirely featureless save for the solid, securely fastened door. Presently he lay down on the deck and gave himself up to fruitless thinking.

He had plenty of time to think, time to fall asleep and awaken more than once. And time to grow very hungry and very, very thirsty.

When Joe-Jim next took sufficient interest in his prisoner to open the door of the cell, Hoyland was not immediately in evidence. He had planned many times what he would do when the door opened and his chance came, but when the event arrived, he was too weak, semi-comatose. Joe-Jim dragged him out.

The disturbance roused him to partial comprehension. He sat up and stared around him.

"Ready to talk?" asked Jim.

Hoyland opened his mouth but no words came out.

"Can't you see he's too dry to talk?" Joe told his twin. Then to Hugh: "Will you talk if we give you some water?"

Hoyland looked puzzled, then nodded vigorously.

Joe-Jim returned in a moment with a mug of water. Hugh drank greedily, paused, and seemed about to faint.

Joe-Jim took the mug from him. "That's enough for now," said Joe. "Tell us about yourself."

Hugh did so. In detail, being prompted from time to time.

Hugh accepted a *de facto* condition of slavery with no particular resistance and no great disturbance of soul. The word "slave" was not in his vocabulary, but the condition was a commonplace in everything he had ever known. There had always been those who gave orders and those who carried them out—he could imagine no other condition, no other type of social organization. It was a fact of nature.

Though naturally he thought of escape.

Thinking about it was as far as he got. Joe-Jim guessed his thoughts and brought the matter out into the open. Joe told him, "Don't go getting ideas, youngster. Without a knife you wouldn't get three levels away in this part of the Ship. If you managed to steal a knife from me, you still wouldn't make it down to high-weight. Besides, there's Bobo."

Hugh waited a moment, as was fitting, then said, "Bobo?"

Jim grinned and replied, "We told Bobo that you were

his to butcher, if he liked, if you ever stuck your head out of our compartments without us. Now he sleeps outside the door and spends a lot of his time there.''

"It was only fair,'' put in Joe. "He was disappointed when we decided to keep you.''

"Say,'' suggested Jim, turning his head toward his brother's, "how about some fun?'' He turned back to Hugh. "Can you throw a knife?''

"Of course,'' Hugh answered.

"Let's see you. Here.'' Joe-Jim handed him their own knife. Hugh accepted it, jiggling it in his hand to try its balance. "Try my mark.''

Joe-Jim had a plastic target set up at the far end of the room from his favorite chair, on which he was wont to practice his own skill. Hugh eyed it, and, with an arm motion too fast to follow, let fly. He used the economical underhand stroke, thumb on the blade, fingers together.

The blade shivered in the target, well centered in the chewed-up area which marked Joe-Jim's best efforts.

"Good boy!'' Joe approved. "What do you have in mind, Jim?''

"Let's give him the knife and see how far he gets.''

"No,'' said Joe, "I don't agree.''

"Why not?''

"If Bobo wins, we're out one servant. If Hugh wins, we lose both Bobo and him. It's wasteful.''

"Oh, well—if you insist.''

"I do. Hugh, fetch the knife.''

Hugh did so. It had not occurred to him to turn the knife against Joe-Jim. The master was the master. For servant to attack master was not simply repugnant to good morals, it was an idea so wild that it did not occur to him at all.

Hugh had expected that Joe-Jim would be impressed by his learning as a scientist. It did not work out that way. Joe-Jim, especially Jim, loved to argue. They sucked Hugh

dry in short order and figuratively cast him aside. Hoyland
felt humiliated. After all, was he not a scientist? Could he
not read and write?

"Shut up," Jim told him. "Reading is simple. I could
do it before your father was born. D'you think you're the
first scientist that has served me? Scientists—bah! A pack
of ignoramuses!"

In an attempt to re-establish his own intellectual con-
ceit, Hugh expounded the theories of the younger scientists, the strictly matter-of-fact, hard-boiled realism which
rejected all religious interpretation and took the Ship as it
was. He confidently expected Joe-Jim to approve such a
point of view; it seemed to fit their temperaments.

They laughed in his face.

"Honest," Jim insisted, when he had ceased snorting,
"are you young punks so stupid as all that? Why, you're
worse than your elders."

"But you just got through saying," Hugh protested in
hurt tones, "that all our accepted religious notions are so
much bunk. That is just what my friends think. They want
to junk all that old nonsense."

Joe started to speak; Jim cut in ahead of him. "Why
bother with him, Joe? He's hopeless."

"No, he's not. I'm enjoying this. He's the first one I've
talked with in I don't know how long who stood any chance
at all of seeing the truth. Let us be—I want to see whether
that's a head he has on his shoulders, or just a place to
hang his ears."

"O.K.," Jim agreed, "but keep it quiet. I'm going to
take a nap." The left-hand head closed its eyes, soon it
was snoring. Joe and Hugh continued their discussion in
whispers.

"The trouble with you youngsters," Joe said, "is that
if you can't understand a thing right off, you think it can't
be true. The trouble with your elders is, anything they
didn't understand they reinterpreted to mean something

else and then thought they understood it. None of you has tried believing clear words the way they were written and then tried to understand them on that basis. Oh, no, you're all too bloody smart for that—if you can't see it right off, it ain't so—it must mean something different.''

"What do you mean?" Hugh asked suspiciously.

"Well, take the Trip, for instance. What does it mean to you?"

"Well—to my mind, it doesn't mean anything. It's just a piece of nonsense to impress the peasants."

"And what is the accepted meaning?"

"Well—it's where you go when you die—or rather what you do. You make the Trip to Centaurus."

"And what is Centaurus?"

"It's—mind you, I'm just telling you the orthodox answers; I don't really believe this stuff—it's where you arrive when you've made the Trip, a place where everybody's happy and there's always good eating."

Joe snorted. Jim broke the rhythm of his snoring, opened one eye, and settled back again with a grunt. "That's just what I mean," Joe went on in a lower whisper. "You don't use your head. Did it ever occur to you that the Trip was just what the old books said it was—the Ship and all the Crew actually going somewhere, moving?"

Hoyland thought about it. "You don't mean for me to take you seriously. Physically, it's an impossibility. The Ship can't *go* anywhere. It already *is* everywhere. We can make a trip through it, but *the* Trip—that has to have a spiritual meaning, if it has any."

Joe called on Jordan to support him. "Now, listen," he said, "get this through that thick head of yours. Imagine a place a lot bigger than the Ship, a lot bigger, with the Ship inside it—*moving*. D'you get it?"

Hugh tried. He tried very hard. He shook his head. "It doesn't make sense," he said. "There can't be anything bigger than the Ship. There wouldn't be any place for it to *be*."

"Oh, for Huff's sake! Listen—*outside* the Ship, get that? Straight down beyond the level in every direction. Emptiness out there. Understand me?"

"But there isn't anything below the lowest level. That's why it's the lowest level."

"Look. If you took a knife and started digging a hole in the floor of the lowest level, where would it get you?"

"But you *can't*. It's too hard."

"But suppose you did and it made a hole. Where would that hole go? Imagine it."

Hugh shut his eyes and tried to imagine digging a hole in the lowest level. Digging—as if it were soft—soft as cheese.

He began to get some glimmering of a possibility, a possibility that was unsettling, soul-shaking. He was falling, falling into a hole that he had dug which had no levels under it. He opened his eyes very quickly. "That's awful!" he ejaculated. "I won't believe it."

Joe-Jim got up. "I'll *make* you believe it," he said grimly, "if I have to break your neck to do it." He strode over to the outer door and opened it. "Bobo!" he shouted. "Bobo!"

Jim's head snapped erect. "Wassa matter? Wha's going on?"

"We're going to take Hugh to no-weight."

"What for?"

"To pound some sense into his silly head."

"Some other time."

"No, I want to do it now."

"All right, all right. No need to shake. I'm awake now, anyhow."

Joe-Jim Gregory was almost as nearly unique in his, or their, mental ability as he was in his bodily construction.

Under any circumstances he would have been a dominant personality; among the muties it was inevitable that he should bully them, order them about, and live on their services. Had he had the will-to-power, it is conceivable that he could have organized the muties to fight and overcome the Crew proper.

But he lacked that drive. He was by native temperament an intellectual, a bystander, an observer. He was interested in the "how" and the "why," but his will to action was satisfied with comfort and convenience alone.

Had he been born two normal twins and among the Crew, it is likely that he would have drifted into scientisthood as the easiest and most satisfactory answer to the problem of living and as such would have entertained himself mildly with conversation and administration. As it was, he lacked mental companionship and had whiled away three generations reading and rereading books stolen for him by his stooges.

The two halves of his dual person had argued and discussed what they had read, and had almost inevitably arrived at a reasonably coherent theory of history and the physical world—except in one respect, the concept of fiction was entirely foreign to them; they treated the novels that had been provided for the Jordan expedition in exactly the same fashion that they did text and reference books.

This led to their one major difference of opinion. Jim regarded Allan Quartermain as the greatest man who had ever lived; Joe held out for John Henry.

They were both inordinately fond of poetry; they could recite page after page of Kipling, and were nearly as fond of Rhysling, "the blind singer of the spaceways."

Bobo backed in. Joe-Jim hooked a thumb toward Hugh. "Look," said Joe, "he's going out."

"Now?" said Bobo happily, and grinned, slavering.

"You and your stomach!" Joe answered, rapping Bobo's pate with his knuckles. "No, you don't eat him. You and him—blood brothers. Get it?"

"Not eat 'im?"

"No. Fight for him. He fights for you."

"O.K." The pinhead shrugged his shoulders at the inevitable. "Blood brothers. Bobo know."

"All right. Now we go up to the place-where-everybody-flies. You go ahead and make lookout."

They climbed in single file, the dwarf running ahead to spot the lie of the land, Hoyland behind him, Joe-Jim bringing up the rear, Joe with eyes to the front, Jim watching their rear, head turned over his shoulder.

Higher and higher they went, weight slipping imperceptibly from them with each successive deck. They emerged finally into a level beyond which there was no further progress, no opening above them. The deck curved gently, suggesting that the true shape of the space was a giant cylinder, but overhead a metallic expanse which exhibited a similar curvature obstructed the view and prevented one from seeing whether or not the deck in truth curved back on itself.

There were no proper bulkheads; great stanchions, so huge and squat as to give an impression of excessive, unnecessary strength, grew thickly about them, spacing deck and overhead evenly apart.

Weight was imperceptible. If one remained quietly in one place, the undetectable residuum of weight would bring the body in a gentle drift down to the "floor," but "up" and "down" were terms largely lacking in meaning. Hugh did not like it; it made him gulp, but Bobo seemed delighted by it and not unused to it. He moved through the air like an uncouth fish, banking off stanchion, floor plate, and overhead as suited his convenience.

Joe-Jim set a course parallel to the common axis of the inner and outer cylinders, following a passageway formed by the orderly spacing of the stanchions. There were hand-

rails set along the passage, one of which he followed like
a spider on its thread. He made remarkable speed, which
Hugh floundered to maintain. In time, he caught the trick
of the easy, effortless, overhand pull, the long coast against
nothing but air resistance, and the occasional flick of the
toes or the hand against the floor. But he was much too
busy to tell how far they went before they stopped. Miles,
he guessed it to be, but he did not know.

When they did stop, it was because the passage had
terminated. A solid bulkhead, stretching away to right and
left, barred their way. Joe-Jim moved along it to the right,
searching.

He found what he sought, a man-sized door, closed, its
presence distinguishable only by a faint crack which
marked its outline and a cursive geometrical design on its
surface. Joe-Jim studied this and scratched his right-hand
head. The two heads whispered to each other. Joe-Jim
raised his hand in an awkward gesture.

"No, no!" said Jim. Joe-Jim checked himself. "How's
that?" Joe answered. They whispered together again, Joe
nodded, and Joe-Jim again raised his hand.

He traced the design on the door without touching it,
moving his forefinger through the air perhaps four inches
from the surface of the door. The order of succession in
which his finger moved over the lines of the design appeared simple but certainly not obvious.

Finished, he shoved a palm against the adjacent bulkhead, drifted back from the door, and waited.

A moment later there was a soft, almost inaudible in-
sufflation; the door stirred and moved outward perhaps six
inches, then stopped. Joe-Jim appeared puzzled. He ran
his hands cautiously into the open crack and pulled. Nothing happened. He called to Bobo, "Open it."

Bobo looked the situation over, with a scowl on his
forehead which wrinkled almost to his crown. He then
placed his feet against the bulkhead, steadying himself by

grasping the door with one hand. He took hold of the edge of the door with both hands, settled his feet firmly, bowed his body, and strained.

He held his breath, chest rigid, back bent, sweat breaking out from the effort. The great cords in his neck stood out, making of his head a misshapen pyramid. Hugh could hear the dwarf's joints crack. It was easy to believe that he would kill himself with the attempt, too stupid to give up.

But the door gave suddenly, with a plaint of binding metal. As the door, in swinging out, slipped from Bobo's fingers, the unexpectedly released tension in his legs shoved him heavily away from the bulkhead; he plunged down the passageway, floundering for a handhold. But he was back in a moment, drifting awkwardly through the air as he massaged a cramped calf.

Joe-Jim led the way inside, Hugh close behind him. "What is this place?" demanded Hugh, his curiosity overcoming his servant manners.

"The Main Control Room," said Joe.

Main Control Room! The most sacred and taboo place in the Ship, its very location a forgotten mystery. In the credo of the young men it was nonexistent. The older scientists varied in their attitude between fundamentalist acceptance and mystical belief. As enlightened as Hugh believed himself to be, the very words frightened him. The Control Room! Why, the very spirit of Jordan was said to reside there.

He stopped.

Joe-Jim stopped and Joe looked around. "Come on," he said. "What's the matter?"

"Why—uh—uh—"

"Speak up."

"But—but this place is haunted—this is Jordan's—"

"Oh, for Jordan's sake!" protested Joe, with slow exasperation. "I thought you told me you young punks didn't take any stock in Jordan."

"Yes, but—but this is—"

"Stow it. Come along, or I'll have Bobo drag you." He turned away. Hugh followed, reluctantly, as a man climbs a scaffold.

They threaded through a passageway just wide enough for two to use the handrails abreast. The passage curved in a wide sweeping arc of full ninety degrees, then opened into the control room proper. Hugh peered past Joe-Jim's broad shoulders, fearful but curious.

He stared into a well-lighted room, huge, quite two hundred feet across. It was spherical, the interior of a great globe. The surface of the globe was featureless, frosted silver. In the geometrical center of the sphere Hugh saw a group of apparatus about fifteen feet across. To his inexperienced eye, it was completely unintelligible; he could not have described it, but he saw that it floated steadily, with no apparent support.

Running from the end of the passage to the mass at the center of the globe was a tube of metal latticework, wide as the passage itself. It offered the only exit from the passage. Joe-Jim turned to Bobo, and ordered him to remain in the passageway, then entered the tube.

He pulled himself along it, hand over hand, the bars of the latticework making a ladder. Hugh followed him; they emerged into the mass of apparatus occupying the center of the sphere. Seen close up, the gear of the control station resolved itself into its individual details, but it still made no sense to him. He glanced away from it to the inner surface of the globe which surrounded them.

That was a mistake. The surface of the globe, being featureless silvery white, had nothing to lend it perspective. It might have been a hundred feet away, or a thousand, or many miles. He had never experienced an unbroken height greater than that between two decks, nor an open space larger than the village common. He was panic-stricken, scared out of his wits, the more so in that he did not know what it was he feared. But the ghost of long-forgotten jungle ancestors possessed him and chilled his stomach with the basic primitive fear of falling.

He clutched at the control gear, clutched at Joe-Jim.

Joe-Jim let him have one, hard across the mouth with the flat of his hand. "What's the matter with you?" growled Jim.

"I don't know," Hugh presently managed to get out. "I don't know, but I don't *like* this place. Let's get out of here!"

Jim lifted his eyebrows to Joe, looked disgusted, and said, "We might as well. That weak-bellied baby will never understand anything you tell him."

"Oh, he'll be all right," Joe replied, dismissing the matter. "Hugh, climb into one of the chairs—there, that one."

In the meantime, Hugh's eyes had fallen on the tube whereby they had reached the control center and had followed it back by eye to the passage door. The sphere suddenly shrank to its proper focus and the worst of his panic was over. He complied with the order, still trembling, but able to obey.

The control center consisted of a rigid framework, made up of chairs, or frames, to receive the bodies of the operators, and consolidated instrument and report panels, mounted in such a fashion as to be almost in the laps of the operators, where they were readily visible but did not obstruct the view. The chairs had high supporting sides, or arms, and mounted in these arms were the controls appropriate to each officer on watch—but Hugh was not yet aware of that.

He slid under the instrument panel into his seat and settled back, glad of its enfolding stability. It fitted him in a semi-reclining position, footrest to head support.

But something was happening on the panel in front of Joe-Jim; he caught it out of the corner of his eye and turned to look. Bright red letters glowed near the top of the board: 2ND ASTROGATOR POSTED. What was a second astrogator? He didn't know—then he noticed that the extreme top of his own board was labeled 2ND ASTROGATOR and concluded it must be himself, or rather, the man who should be sitting there. He felt momentarily uncomfortable that the proper second astrogator might come in and find him usurping his post, but he put it out of his mind—it seemed unlikely.

But what was a second astrogator, anyhow?

The letters faded from Joe-Jim's board, a red dot appeared on the left-hand edge and remained. Joe-Jim did something with his right hand; his board reported: AC-CELERATION—ZERO, then MAIN DRIVE. The last two words blinked several times, then were replaced with NO REPORT. These words faded out, and a bright green dot appeared near the right-hand edge.

"Get ready," said Joe, looking toward Hugh; "the light is going out."

"You're not going to turn out the light?" protested Hugh.

"No—you are. Take a look by your left hand. See those little white lights?"

Hugh did so, and found, shining up through the surface of the chair arm, eight bright little beads of light arranged in two squares, one above the other.

"Each one controls the light of one quadrant," explained Joe. "Cover them with your hand to turn out the light. Go ahead—do it."

Reluctantly, but fascinated, Hugh did as he was directed. He placed a palm over the tiny lights, and waited. The silvery sphere turned to dull lead, faded still more, leaving them in darkness complete save for the silent glow from the instrument panels. Hugh felt nervous but exhilarated. He withdrew his palm; the sphere remained dark, the eight little lights had turned blue.

"Now," said Joe, "I'm going to show you the stars!"

In the darkness, Joe-Jim's right hand slid over another pattern of eight lights.

Creation.

Faithfully reproduced, shining as steady and serene from the walls of the stellarium as did their originals from the black deeps of space, the mirrored stars looked down on him. Light after jeweled light, scattered in careless bountiful splendor across the simulacrum sky, the countless suns lay before him—before him, over him, under him, behind him, in every direction from him. He hung alone in the center of the stellar universe.

"Oooooh!" It was an involuntary sound, caused by his indrawn breath. He clutched the chair arms hard enough to break fingernails, but he was not aware of it. Nor was he afraid at the moment; there was room in his being for but one emotion. Life within the Ship, alternately harsh and workaday, had placed no strain on his innate capacity to experience beauty; for the first time in his life he knew the intolerable ecstasy of beauty unalloyed. It shook him and hurt him, like the first trembling intensity of sex.

It was some time before Hugh sufficiently recovered from the shock and the ensuing intense preoccupation to be able to notice Jim's sardonic laugh, Joe's dry chuckle. "Had enough?" inquired Joe. Without waiting for a reply, Joe-Jim turned the lights back on, using the duplicate controls mounted in the left arm of his chair.

Hugh sighed. His chest ached and his heart pounded. He realized suddenly that he had been holding his breath the entire time that the lights had been turned out. "Well, smart boy," asked Jim, "are you convinced?"

Hugh sighed again, not knowing why. With the lights back on, he felt safe and snug again, but was possessed of a deep sense of personal loss. He knew, subconsciously, that, having seen the stars, he would never be happy again. The dull ache in his breast, the vague inchoate yearning for his lost heritage of open sky and stars, was never to be silenced, even though he was yet too ignorant to be aware of it at the top of his mind. "What was it?" he asked in a hushed voice.

"That's *it*," answered Joe. "That's the world. That's the universe. That's what I've been trying to tell you about."

Hugh tried furiously to force his inexperienced mind to comprehend. "That's what you mean by Outside?" he asked. "All those beautiful little lights?"

"Sure," said Joe, "only they aren't little. They're a long way off, you see—maybe thousands of miles." .

"What?"

"Sure, sure," Joe persisted. "There's lots of room out there. Space. It's big. Why, some of those stars may be as big as the Ship—maybe bigger."

Hugh's face was a pitiful study in overstrained imagination. "Bigger than the Ship?" he repeated. "But—but—"

Jim tossed his head impatiently and said to Joe, "Wha'd' I tell you? You're wasting our time on this lunk. He hasn't got the capacity—"

"Easy, Jim," Joe answered mildly; "don't expect him to run before he can crawl. It took us a long time. I seem to remember that you were a little slow to believe your own eyes."

"That's a lie," said Jim nastily. "*You* were the one that had to be convinced."

"O.K., O.K.," Joe conceded, "let it ride. But it was a long time before we both had it all straight."

Hoyland paid little attention to the exchange between the two brothers. It was a usual thing; his attention was centered on matters decidedly not usual. "Joe," he asked, "what became of the Ship while we were looking at the stars? Did we stare right through it?"

"Not exactly," Joe told him. "You weren't looking directly at the stars at all, but at a kind of picture of them. It's like— Well, they do it with mirrors, sort of. I've got a book that tells about it."

"But you *can* see 'em directly," volunteered Jim, his momentary pique forgotten. "There's a compartment forward of here—"

"Oh, yes," put in Joe, "it slipped my mind. The Captain's veranda. 'S got one all of glass; you can look right out."

"The Captain's veranda? But—"

"Not *this* Captain. He's never been near the place. That's the name over the door of the compartment."

"What's a 'veranda'?"

"Blessed if I know. It's just the name of the place."

"Will you take me up there?"

Joe appeared to be about to agree, but Jim cut in. "Some other time. I want to get back—I'm hungry."

They passed back through the tube, woke up Bobo, and made the long trip back down.

It was long before Hugh could persuade Joe-Jim to take him exploring again, but the time intervening was well spent. Joe-Jim turned him loose on the largest collection of books that Hugh had ever seen. Some of them were copies of books Hugh had seen before, but even these he read with new meanings. He read incessantly, his mind soaking up new ideas, stumbling over them, struggling, striving to grasp them. He begrudged sleep, he forgot to eat until his breath grew sour and compelling pain in his midriff forced him to pay attention to his body. Hunger satisfied, he would be back at it until his head ached and his eyes refused to focus.

Joe-Jim's demands for service were few. Although Hugh

was never off duty, Joe-Jim did not mind his reading as long as he was within earshot and ready to jump when called. Playing checkers with one of the pair when the other did not care to play was the service which used up the most time, and even this was not a total loss, for, if the player were Joe, he could almost always be diverted into a discussion of the Ship, its history, its machinery and equipment, the sort of people who had built it and first manned it—and *their* history, back on Earth, Earth the incredible, that strange place where people had lived on the *outside* instead of the *inside*.

Hugh wondered why they did not fall off.

He took the matter up with Joe and at last gained some notion of gravitation. He never really understood it emotionally—it was too wildly improbable—but as an intellectual concept he was able to accept it and use it, much later, in his first vague glimmerings of the science of ballistics and the art of astrogation and ship maneuvering. And it led in time to his wondering about weight in the Ship, a matter that had never bothered him before. The lower the level the greater the weight had been to his mind simply the order of nature, and nothing to wonder at. He was familiar with centrifugal force as it applied to slingshots. To apply it also to the whole Ship, to think of the Ship as spinning like a slingshot and thereby causing weight, was too much of a hurdle—he never really believed it.

Joe-Jim took him back once more to the Control Room and showed him what little Joe-Jim knew about the manipulation of the controls and the reading of the astrogation instruments.

The long-forgotten engineer-designers employed by the Jordan Foundation had been instructed to design a ship that would not—*could* not—wear out, even though the Trip were protracted beyond the expected sixty years. They builded better than they knew. In planning the main drive engines and the auxiliary machinery, largely automatic, which would make the Ship habitable, and in designing the controls necessary to handle all machinery not entirely automatic, the very idea of moving parts had been rejected. The engines and auxiliary equipment worked on a level below mechanical motion, on a level of pure force, as electrical transformers do. Instead of push buttons, levers, cams, and shafts, the controls and the machinery they served were planned in terms of balance between static fields, bias of electronic flow, circuits broken or closed by a hand placed over a light.

On this level of action, friction lost its meaning, wear and erosion took no toll. Had all hands been killed in the mutiny, the Ship would still have plunged on through space, still lighted, its air still fresh and moist, its engines ready and waiting. As it was, though elevators and conveyor belts fell into disrepair, disuse, and finally into the oblivion of forgotten function, the essential machinery of the Ship continued its automatic service to its ignorant human freight, or waited, quiet and ready, for someone bright enough to puzzle out its key.

Genius had gone into the building of the Ship. Far too huge to be assembled on Earth, it had been put together piece by piece in its own orbit out beyond the Moon. There it had swung for fifteen silent years while the problems presented by the decision to make its machinery foolproof and enduring had been formulated and solved. A whole new field of submolar action had been conceived in the process, struggled with, and conquered.

So— When Hugh placed an untutored, questing hand over the first of a row of lights marked ACCELERATION, POSITIVE, he got an immediate response, though not in terms of acceleration. A red light at the top of the chief pilot's board blinked rapidly and the annunciator panel glowed with a message: MAIN ENGINES—NOT MANNED.

"What does that mean?" he asked Joe-Jim.

"There's no telling," said Jim. "We've done the same thing in the main engine room," added Joe. "There, when you try it, it says 'Control Room Not Manned.'"

Hugh thought a moment. "What would happen," he persisted, "if all the control stations had somebody at 'em at once, and then I did that?"

"Can't say," said Joe. "Never been able to try it."

Hugh said nothing. A resolve which had been growing, formless, in his mind was now crystallizing into decision. He was busy with it.

He waited until he found Joe-Jim in a mellow mood, both of him, before broaching his idea. They were in the Captain's veranda at the time Hugh decided the moment was ripe. Joe-Jim rested gently in the Captain's easy chair, his belly full of food, and gazed out through the heavy glass of the view port at the serene stars. Hugh floated beside him. The spinning of the Ship caused the stars to appear to move in stately circles.

Presently he said, "Joe-Jim—"

"Eh? What's that, youngster?" It was Joe who had replied.

"It's pretty swell, isn't it?"

"What is?"

"All that. The stars." Hugh indicated the view through the port with a sweep of his arm, then caught at the chair to stop his own backspin.

"Yeah, it sure is. Makes you feel good." Surprisingly, it was Jim who offered this.

Hugh knew the time was right. He waited a moment, then said, "Why don't we finish the job?"

Two heads turned simultaneously, Joe leaning out a little to see past Jim. "What job?"

"The Trip. Why don't we start up the main drive and go on with it? Somewhere out there," he said hurriedly to finish before he was interrupted, "there are planets like Earth—or so the First Crew thought. Let's go find them."

Jim looked at him, then laughed. Joe shook his head.

"Kid," he said, "you don't know what you are talking about. You're as balmy as Bobo. No," he went on, "that's all over and done with. Forget it."

"Why is it over and done with, Joe?"

"Well, because— It's too big a job. It takes a crew that understands what it's all about, trained to operate the Ship."

"Does it take so many? You have shown me only about a dozen places, all told, for men actually to be at the controls. Couldn't a dozen men run the Ship—if they knew what you know," he added slyly.

Jim chuckled. "He's got you, Joe. He's right."

Joe brushed it aside. "You overrate our knowledge. Maybe we *could* operate the Ship, but we wouldn't get anywhere. We don't know where we are. The Ship has been drifting for I don't know how many generations. We don't know where we're headed, or how fast we're going."

"But look," Hugh pleaded, "there are instruments. You showed them to me. Couldn't we learn how to use them? Couldn't *you* figure them out, Joe, if you really wanted to?"

"Oh, I suppose so," Jim agreed.

"Don't boast, Jim," said Joe.

"I'm not boasting," snapped Jim. "If a thing'll work, I can figure it out."

"Humph!" said Joe.

The matter rested in delicate balance. Hugh had got them disagreeing among themselves—which was what he wanted—with the less tractable of the pair on his side. Now, to consolidate his gain—

"I had an idea," he said quickly, "to get you men to work with, Jim, if you were able to train them."

"What's your idea?" demanded Jim suspiciously.

"Well, you remember what I told you about a bunch of the younger scientists—"

"Those fools!"

"Yes, yes, sure—but they don't know what you know. In their way they were trying to be reasonable. Now, if I could go back down and tell them what you've taught me, I could get you enough men to work with."

Joe cut in. "Take a good look at us, Hugh. What do you see?"

"Why—why—I see *you*—Joe-Jim."

"You see a mutie," corrected Joe, his voice edged with sarcasm. "We're a *mutie*. Get that? Your scientists won't work with us."

"No, no," protested Hugh, "that's not true. I'm not talking about peasants. Peasants wouldn't understand, but these are *scientists*, and the smartest of the lot. They'll understand. All you need to do is to arrange safe conduct for them through mutie country. You can do that, can't you?" he added, instinctively shifting the point of the argument to firmer ground.

"Why, sure," said Jim.

"Forget it," said Joe.

"Well, O.K.," Hugh agreed, sensing that Joe really was annoyed at his persistence, "but it would be fun—" He withdrew some distance from the brothers.

He could hear Joe-Jim continuing the discussion with himself in low tones. He pretended to ignore it. Joe-Jim had this essential defect in his joint nature: being a committee, rather than a single individual, he was hardly fitted to be a man of action, since all decisions were necessarily the result of discussion and compromise.

Several moments later Hugh heard Joe's voice raised. "All right, all *right*—have it your own way!" He then called out, "Hugh! Come here!"

Hugh kicked himself away from an adjacent bulkhead

and shot over to the immediate vicinity of Joe-Jim, arresting his flight with both hands against the framework of the Captain's chair.

"We've decided," said Joe without preliminaries, "to let you go back down to the high-weight and try to peddle your goods. But you're a fool," he added sourly.

Bobo escorted Hugh down through the dangers of the levels frequented by muties and left him in the uninhabited zone above high-weight. "Thanks, Bobo," Hugh said in parting. "Good eating." The dwarf grinned, ducked his head, and sped away, swarming up the ladder they had just descended.

Hugh turned and started down, touching his knife as he did so. It was good to feel it against him again. Not that it was his original knife. That had been Bobo's prize when he was captured, and Bobo had been unable to return it, having inadvertently left it sticking in a big one that got away. But the replacement Joe-Jim had given him was well balanced and quite satisfactory.

Bobo had conducted him, at Hugh's request and by Joe-Jim's order, down to the area directly over the auxiliary Converter used by the scientists. He wanted to find Bill Ertz, Assistant Chief Engineer and leader of the bloc of younger scientists, and he did not want to have to answer too many questions before he found him.

Hugh dropped quickly down the remaining levels and found himself in a main passageway which he recognized. Good! A turn to the left, a couple of hundred yards' walk and he found himself at the door of the compartment which housed the Converter. A guard lounged in front of it. Hugh started to push on past, was stopped. "Where do you think you're going?"

"I want to find Bill Ertz."

"You mean the Chief Engineer? Well, he's not here."

"Chief? What's happened to the old one?" Hoyland regretted the remark at once—but it was already out.

"Huh? The old Chief? Why, he's made the Trip long since." The guard looked at him suspiciously. "What's wrong with you?"

"Nothing," denied Hugh. "Just a slip."

"Funny sort of a slip. Well, you'll find Chief Ertz around his office probably."

"Thanks. Good eating."

"Good eating."

Hugh was admitted to see Ertz after a short wait. Ertz looked up from his desk as Hugh came in. "Well," he said, "so you're back, and not dead after all. This *is* a surprise. We had written you off, you know, as making the Trip."

"Yes, I suppose so."

"Well, sit down and tell me about it—I've a little time to spare at the moment. Do you know, though, I wouldn't have recognized you. You've changed a lot—all that gray hair. I imagine you had some pretty tough times."

Gray hair? Was his hair gray? And Ertz had changed a lot, too, Hugh now noticed. He was paunchy and the lines in his face had set. Good Jordan! How long had he been gone?

Ertz drummed on his desk top, and pursed his lips. "It makes a problem—your coming back like this. I'm afraid I can't just assign you to your old job; Mort Tyler has that. But we'll find a place for you, suitable to your rank."

Hugh recalled Mort Tyler and not too favorably. A precious sort of a chap, always concerned with what was proper and according to regulations. So Tyler had actually made scientisthood, and was on Hugh's old job at the Converter. Well, it didn't matter. "That's all right," he began. "I wanted to talk to you about—"

"Of course, there's the matter of seniority," Ertz went on. "Perhaps the Council had better consider the matter.

I don't know of a precedent. We've lost a number of scientists to the muties in the past, but you are the first to escape with his life in my memory."

"That doesn't matter," Hugh broke in. "I've something much more pressing to talk about. While I was away I found out some amazing things, Bill, things that it is of paramount importance for you to know about. That's why I came straight to you. Listen, I—"

Ertz was suddenly alert. "Of course you have! I must be slowing down. You must have had a marvelous opportunity to study the muties and scout out their territory. Come on, man, spill it! Give me your report."

Hugh wet his lips. "It's not what you think," he said. "It's much more important than just a report on the muties, though it concerns them, too. In fact, we may have to change our whole policy with respect to the mu—"

"Well, go ahead, go ahead! I'm listening."

"All right." Hugh told him of his tremendous discovery as to the actual nature of the Ship, choosing his words carefully and trying very hard to be convincing. He dwelt lightly on the difficulties presented by an attempt to reorganize the Ship in accordance with the new concept and bore down heavily on the prestige and honor that would accrue to the man who led the effort.

He watched Ertz's face as he talked. After the first start of complete surprise when Hugh launched his key idea, the fact that the Ship was actually a moving body in a great outside space, his face became impassive and Hugh could read nothing in it, except that he seemed to detect a keener interest when Hugh spoke of how Ertz was just the man for the job because of his leadership of the younger, more progressive scientists.

When Hugh concluded, he waited for Ertz's response. Ertz said nothing at first, simply continued with his annoying habit of drumming on the top of his desk. Finally he said, "These are important matters, Hoyland, much too important to be dealt with casually. I must have time to chew it over."

"Yes, certainly," Hugh agreed. "I wanted to add that I've made arrangements for safe passage up to no-weight. I can take you up and let you see for yourself."

"No doubt that is best," Ertz replied. "Well—are you hungry?"

"No."

"Then we'll both sleep on it. You can use the compartment at the back of my office. I don't want you discussing this with anyone else until I've had time to think about it; it might cause unrest if it got out without proper preparation."

"Yes, you're right."

"Very well, then"—Ertz ushered him into a compartment behind his office which he very evidently used for a lounge—"have a good rest," he said, "and we'll talk later."

"Thanks," Hugh acknowledged. "Good eating."

"Good eating."

Once he was alone, Hugh's excitement gradually dropped away from him, and he realized that he was fagged out and very sleepy. He stretched out on a built-in couch and fell asleep.

When he awoke he discovered that the only door to the compartment was barred from the other side. Worse than that, his knife was gone.

He had waited an indefinitely long time when he heard activity at the door. It opened; two husky, unsmiling men entered. "Come along," said one of them. He sized them up, noting that neither of them carried a knife. No chance to snatch one from their belts, then. On the other hand he might be able to break away from them.

But beyond them, a wary distance away in the outer room, were two other equally formidable men, each armed with a knife. One balanced his for throwing; the other held his by the grip, ready to stab at close quarters.

He was boxed in and he knew it. They had anticipated his possible moves.

He had long since learned to relax before the inevitable. He composed his face and marched quietly out. Once through the door he saw Ertz, waiting and quite evidently in charge of the party of men. He spoke to him, being careful to keep his voice calm. "Hello, Bill. Pretty extensive preparations you've made. Some trouble, maybe?"

Ertz seemed momentarily uncertain of his answer, then said, "You're going before the Captain."

"Good!" Hugh answered. "Thanks, Bill. But do you think it's wise to try to sell the idea to him without laying a little preliminary foundation with the others?"

Ertz was annoyed at his apparent thickheadedness and showed it. "You don't get the idea," he growled. "You're going before the Captain to stand trial—for heresy!"

Hugh considered this as if the idea had not before occurred to him. He answered mildly, "You're off down the wrong passage, Bill. Perhaps a charge and trial is the best way to get at the matter, but I'm not a peasant, simply to be hustled before the Captain. I must be tried by the Council. I am a scientist."

"Are you now?" Ertz said softly. "I've had advice about that. You were written off the lists. Just what you are is a matter for the Captain to determine."

Hugh held his peace. It was against him, he could see, and there was no point in antagonizing Ertz. Ertz made a signal; the two unarmed men each grasped one of Hugh's arms. He went with them quietly.

Hugh looked at the Captain with new interest. The old man had not changed much—a little fatter, perhaps.

The Captain settled himself slowly down in his chair, and picked up the memorandum before him.

"What's this all about?" he began irritably. "I don't understand it."

Mort Tyler was there to present the case against Hugh, a circumstance which Hugh had had no way of anticipating and which added to his misgivings. He searched his boyhood recollections for some handle by which to reach the man's sympathy, found none. Tyler cleared his throat and commenced:

"This is the case of one Hugh Hoyland, Captain, formerly one of your junior scientists—"

"Scientist, eh? Why doesn't the Council deal with him?"

"Because he is no longer a scientist, Captain. He went over to the muties. He now returns among us, preaching heresy and seeking to undermine your authority."

The Captain looked at Hugh with the ready belligerency of a man jealous of his prerogatives.

"Is that so?" he bellowed. "What have you to say for yourself?"

"It is not true, Captain," Hugh answered. "All that I have said to anyone has been an affirmation of the absolute truth of our ancient knowledge. I have not disputed the truths under which we live; I have simply affirmed them more forcibly than is the ordinary custom. I—"

"I still don't understand this," the Captain interrupted, shaking his head. "You're charged with heresy, yet you say you believe the Teachings. If you aren't guilty, why are you here?"

"Perhaps I can clear the matter up," put in Ertz. "Hoyland—"

"Well, I hope you can," the Captain went on. "Come— let's hear it."

Ertz proceeded to give a reasonably correct, but slanted, version of Hoyland's return and his strange story. The Captain listened, with an expression that varied between puzzlement and annoyance.

When Ertz had concluded, the Captain turned to Hugh. "Humph!" he said.

Hugh spoke immediately. "The gist of my contention, Captain, is that there is a place up at no-weight where you can actually *see* the truth of our faith that the Ship is moving, where you can actually see Jordan's Plan in operation. That is not a denial of faith; that affirms it. There is no need to take my word for it. Jordan Himself will prove it."

Seeing that the Captain appeared to be in a state of indecision, Tyler broke in: "Captain, there is a possible explanation of this incredible situation which I feel duty bound that you should hear. Offhand, there are two obvious interpretations of Hoyland's ridiculous story: He may simply be guilty of extreme heresy, or he may be a mutie at heart and engaged in a scheme to lure you into their hands. But there is a third, more charitable explanation and one which I feel within me is probably the true one.

"There is record that Hoyland was seriously considered for the Converter at his birth inspection, but that his deviation from normal was slight, being simply an overlarge head, and he was passed. It seems to me that the terrible experiences he has undergone at the hands of the muties have finally unhinged an unstable mind. The poor chap is simply not responsible for his own actions."

Hugh looked at Tyler with new respect. To absolve him of guilt and at the same time to make absolutely certain that Hugh would wind up making the Trip—how neat!

The Captain shook a palm at them. "This has gone on long enough." Then, turning to Ertz: "Is there recommendation?"

"Yes, Captain. The Converter."

"Very well, then. I really don't see, Ertz," he continued testily, "why I should be bothered with these details. It seems to me that you should be able to handle discipline in your department without my help."

"Yes, Captain."

The Captain shoved back from his desk, started to get up. "Recommendation confirmed. Dismissed."

Anger flooded through Hugh at the unreasonable injustice of it. They had not even considered looking at the only real evidence he had in his defense. He heard a shout: "Wait!"—then discovered it was his own voice.

The Captain paused, looking at him.

"Wait a moment," Hugh went on, his words spilling out of their own accord. "This won't make any difference, for you're all so damn sure you know all the answers that you won't consider a fair offer to come see with your own eyes. Nevertheless— Nevertheless—it *still* moves!"

Hugh had plenty of time to think, lying in the compartment where they confined him to await the power needs of the Converter, time to think, and to second-guess his mistakes. Telling his tale to Ertz immediately—that had been mistake number one. He should have waited, become reacquainted with the man and felt him out, instead of depending on a friendship which had never been very close.

Second mistake, Mort Tyler. When he heard his name he should have investigated and found out just how much influence the man had with Ertz. He had known him of old, he should have known better.

Well, here he was, condemned as a mutant—or maybe as a heretic. It came to the same thing. He considered whether or not he should have tried to explain why mutants happened. He had learned about it himself in some of the old records in Joe-Jim's possession. No, it wouldn't wash. How could you explain about radiations from the Outside causing the birth of mutants when the listeners did not believe there was such a place as Outside? No, he had messed it up before he was ever taken before the Captain.

His self-recriminations were disturbed at last by the

sound of his door being unfastened. It was too soon for another of the infrequent meals; he thought that they had come at last to take him away, and renewed his resolve to take someone with him.

But he was mistaken. He heard a voice of gentle dignity: "Son, son, how does this happen?" It was Lieutenant Nelson, his first teacher, looking older than ever and frail.

The interview was distressing for both of them. The old man, childless himself, had cherished great hopes for his protégé, even the ambition that he might eventually aspire to the captaincy, though he had kept his vicarious ambition to himself, believing it not good for the young to praise them too highly. It had hurt his heart when the youth was lost.

Now he had returned, a man, but under disgraceful conditions and under sentence of death.

The meeting was no less unhappy for Hugh. He had loved the old man, in his way, wanted to please him and needed his approval. But he could see, as he told his story, that Nelson was not capable of treating the story as anything but an aberration of Hugh's mind, and he suspected that Nelson would rather see him meet a quick death in the Converter, his atoms smashed to hydrogen and giving up clean useful power, than have him live to make a mock of the ancient teachings.

In that he did the old man an injustice; he underrated Nelson's mercy, but not his devotion to "science." But let it be said for Hugh that, had there been no more at issue than his own personal welfare, he might have preferred death to breaking the heart of his benefactor—being a romantic and more than a bit foolish.

Presently the old man got up to leave, the visit having grown unendurable to each of them. "Is there anything I can do for you, son? Do they feed you well enough?"

"Quite well, thanks," Hugh lied.

"Is there anything else?"

"No—yes, you might send me some tobacco. I haven't had a chew in a long time."

"I'll take care of it. Is there anyone you would like to see?"

"Why, I was under the impression that I was not permitted visitors—ordinary visitors."

"You are right, but I think perhaps I may be able to get the rule relaxed. But you will have to give me your promise not to speak of your heresy," he added anxiously.

Hugh thought quickly. This was a new aspect, a new possibility. His uncle? No, while they had always got along well, their minds did not meet—they would greet each other as strangers. He had never made friends easily; Ertz had been his obvious next friend and now look at the damned thing! Then he recalled his village chum, Alan Mahoney, with whom he had played as a boy. True, he had seen practically nothing of him since the time he was apprenticed to Nelson. Still—

"Does Alan Mahoney still live in our village?"

"Why, yes."

"I'd like to see him, if he'll come."

Alan arrived, nervous, ill at ease, but plainly glad to see Hugh and very much upset to find him under sentence to make the Trip. Hugh pounded him on the back. "Good boy," he said. "I knew you would come."

"Of course, I would," protested Alan, "once I knew. But nobody in the village knew it. I don't think even the Witnesses knew it."

"Well, you're here, that's what matters. Tell me about yourself. Have you married?"

"Huh, uh, no. Let's not waste time talking about me. Nothing ever happens to me anyhow. How in Jordan's name did you get in this jam, Hugh?"

"I can't talk about that, Alan. I promised Lieutenant Nelson that I wouldn't."

"Well, what's a promise—*that* kind of a promise? You're in a *jam*, fellow."

"Don't I know it!"

"Somebody have it in for you?"

"Well—our old pal Mort Tyler didn't help any; I think I can say that much."

Alan whistled and nodded his head slowly. "That explains a lot."

"How come? You know something?"

"Maybe, maybe not. After you went away he married Edris Baxter."

"So? Hm-m-m—yes, that clears up a lot." He remained silent for a time.

Presently Alan spoke up: "Look, Hugh. You're not going to sit here and take it, are you? Particularly with Tyler mixed in it. We gotta get you outa here."

"How?"

"I don't know. Pull a raid, maybe. I guess I could get a few knives to rally round and help us—all good boys, spoiling for a fight."

"Then, when it's over, we'd all be for the Converter. You, me, and your pals. No, it won't wash."

"But we've *got* to do something. We can't just sit here and wait for them to burn you."

"I know that." Hugh studied Alan's face. Was it a fair thing to ask? He went on, reassured by what he had seen. "Listen. You would do anything you could to get me out of this, wouldn't you?"

"You know that." Alan's tone showed hurt.

"Very well, then. There is a dwarf named Bobo. I'll tell you how to find him—"

Alan climbed, up and up, higher than he had ever been since Hugh had led him, as a boy, into foolhardy peril. He was older now, more conservative; he had no stomach for it. To the very real danger of leaving the well-traveled lower levels was added his superstitious ignorance. But still he climbed.

This should be about the place—unless he had lost count. But he saw nothing of the dwarf.

Bobo saw him first. A slingshot load caught Alan in the pit of the stomach, even as he was shouting, "Bobo!"

Bobo backed into Joe-Jim's compartment and dumped his load at the feet of the twins. "Fresh meat," he said proudly.

"So it is," agreed Jim indifferently. "Well, it's yours; take it away."

The dwarf dug a thumb into a twisted ear. "Funny," he said, "he knows Bobo's name."

Joe looked up from the book he was reading—Browning's *Collected Poems*, L-Press, New York, London, Luna City, cr. 35. "That's interesting. Hold on a moment."

Hugh had prepared Alan for the shock of Joe-Jim's appearance. In reasonably short order he collected his wits sufficiently to be able to tell his tale. Joe-Jim listened to it without much comment, Bobo with interest but little comprehension.

When Alan concluded, Jim remarked, "Well, you win, Joe. He didn't make it." Then, turning to Alan, he added, "You can take Hoyland's place. Can you play checkers?"

Alan looked from one head to the other. "But you don't understand," he said. "Aren't you going to do anything about it?"

Joe looked puzzled. "Us? Why should we?"

"But you've *got* to. Don't you see? He's depending on you. There's nobody else he can look to. That's why I came. Don't you see?"

"Wait a moment," drawled Jim, "wait a moment. Keep your belt on. Supposing we did want to help him—which we don't—how in Jordan's Ship could we? Answer me that."

"Why—why—" Alan stumbled in the face of such stupidity. "Why, get up a rescue party, of course, and go down and get him out!"

"Why should we get ourselves killed in a fight to rescue your friend?"

Bobo pricked his ears. "Fight?" he inquired eagerly.

"No, Bobo," Joe denied. "No fight. Just talk."

"Oh," said Bobo and returned to passivity.

Alan looked at the dwarf. "If you'd even let Bobo and me—"

"No," Joe said shortly. "It's out of the question. Shut up about it."

Alan sat in a corner, hugging his knees in despair. If only he could get out of there. He could still try to stir up some help down below. The dwarf seemed to be asleep, though it was difficult to be sure with him. If only Joe-Jim would sleep, too.

Joe-Jim showed no indication of sleepiness. Joe tried to continue reading, but Jim interrupted him from time to time. Alan could not hear what they were saying.

Presently Joe raised his voice. "Is that your idea of fun?" he demanded.

"Well," said Jim, "it beats checkers."

"It does, does it? Suppose you get a knife in your eye— where would I be then?"

"You're getting old, Joe. No juice in you any more."

"You're as old as I am."

"Yeah, but I got young ideas."

"Oh, you make me sick. Have it your own way—but don't blame me. Bobo!"

The dwarf sprang up at once, alert. "Yeah, Boss."

"Go out and dig up Squatty and Long Arm and Pig." Joe-Jim got up, went to a locker, and started pulling knives out of their racks.

Hugh heard the commotion in the passageway outside his prison. It could be the guards coming to take him to the Converter, though they probably wouldn't be so noisy. Or it could be just some excitement unrelated to him. On the other hand it might be—

It was. The door burst open, and Alan was inside, shouting at him and thrusting a brace of knives into his hands. He was hurried out of the door, while stuffing the knives in his belt and accepting two more.

Outside he saw Joe-Jim, who did not see him at once, as he was methodically letting fly, as calmly as if he had been engaging in target practice in his own study. And Bobo, who ducked his head and grinned with a mouth widened by a bleeding cut, but continued the easy flow of the motion whereby he loaded and let fly. There were three others, two of whom Hugh recognized as belonging to Joe-Jim's privately owned gang of bullies—muties by definition and birthplace; they were not deformed.

The count does not include still forms on the floor plates.

"Come on!" yelled Alan. "There'll be more in no time." He hurried down the passage to the right.

Joe-Jim desisted and followed him. Hugh let one blade go for luck at a figure running away to the left. The target was poor, and he had no time to see if he had drawn blood. They scrambled along the passage, Bobo bringing up the rear, as if reluctant to leave the fun, and came to a point where a side passage crossed the main one.

Alan led them to the right again. "Stairs ahead," he shouted.

They did not reach them. An airtight door, rarely used, clanged in their faces ten yards short of the stairs. Joe-Jim's bravoes checked their flight and they looked doubtfully at their master. Bobo broke his thickened nails trying to get a purchase on the door.

The sounds of pursuit were clear behind them.

"Boxed in," said Joe softly. "I hope you like it, Jim."

Hugh saw a head appear around the corner of the passage they had quitted. He threw overhand but the distance was too great; the knife clanged harmlessly against steel. The head disappeared. Long Arm kept his eye on the spot, his sling loaded and ready.

Hugh grabbed Bobo's shoulder. "Listen! Do you see that light?"

The dwarf blinked stupidly. Hugh pointed to the intersection of the glowtubes where they crossed in the overhead directly above the junction of the passages. "That light. Can you hit them where they cross?"

Bobo measured the distance with his eye. It would be a hard shot under any conditions at that range. Here, constricted as he was by the low passageway, it called for a fast, flat trajectory, and allowance for higher weight than he was used to.

He did not answer. Hugh felt the wind of his swing but did not see the shot. There was a tinkling crash; the passage became dark.

"Now!" yelled Hugh, and led them away at a run. As they neared the intersection he shouted, "Hold your breaths! Mind the gas!" The radioactive vapor poured lazily out from the broken tube above and filled the crossing with a greenish mist.

Hugh ran to the right, thankful for his knowledge as an engineer of the lighting circuits. He had picked the right direction; the passage ahead was black, being serviced from beyond the break. He could hear footsteps around him; whether they were friend or enemy he did not know.

They burst into light. No one was in sight but a scared and harmless peasant who scurried away at an unlikely pace. They took a quick muster. All were present, but Bobo was making heavy going of it.

Joe looked at him. "He sniffed the gas, I think. Pound his back."

Pig did so with a will. Bobo belched deeply, was suddenly sick, then grinned.

"He'll do," decided Joe.

The slight delay had enabled one at least to catch up with them. He came plunging out of the dark, unaware of, or careless of, the strength against him. Alan knocked Pig's arm down, as he raised it to throw.

"Let me at 'im!" he demanded. "He's mine!"

It was Tyler.

"Man-fight?" Alan challenged, thumb on his blade.

Tyler's eyes darted from adversary to adversary and accepted the invitation to individual duel by lunging at Alan. The quarters were too cramped for throwing; they closed, each achieving his grab in parry, fist to wrist.

Alan was stockier, probably stronger; Tyler was slippery. He attempted to give Alan a knee to the crotch. Alan evaded it, stamped on Tyler's planted foot. They went down. There was a crunching crack.

A moment later, Alan was wiping his knife against his thigh. "Let's get goin'," he complained. "I'm scared."

They reached a stairway, and raced up it, Long Arm and Pig ahead to fan out on each level and cover their flanks, and the third of the three choppers—Hugh heard him called Squatty—covering the rear. The others bunched in between.

Hugh thought they had won free, when he heard shouts and the clatter of a thrown knife just above him. He reached the level above in time to be cut not deeply but jaggedly by a ricocheted blade.

Three men were down. Long Arm had a blade sticking in the fleshy part of his upper arm, but it did not seem to bother him. His slingshot was still spinning. Pig was scrambling after a thrown knife, his own armament exhausted. But there were signs of his work; one man was down on one knee some twenty feet away. He was bleeding from a knife wound in the thigh.

As the figure steadied himself with one hand against the

bulkhead and reached toward an empty belt with the other, Hugh recognized him.

Bill Ertz.

He had led a party up another way and flanked them, to his own ruin. Bobo crowded behind Hugh and got his mighty arm free for the cast. Hugh caught at it. "Easy, Bobo," he directed. "In the stomach, and easy."

The dwarf looked puzzled, but did as he was told. Ertz folded over at the middle and slid to the deck.

"Well placed," said Jim.

"Bring him along, Bobo," directed Hugh, "and stay in the middle." He ran his eye over their party, now huddled at the top of that flight of stairs. "All right, gang—up we go again! Watch it."

Long Arm and Pig swarmed up the next flight, the others disposing themselves as usual. Joe looked annoyed. In some fashion—a fashion by no means clear at the moment—he had been eased out as leader of this gang—*his* gang—and Hugh was giving orders. He reflected that there was no time now to make a fuss. It might get them all killed.

Jim did not appear to mind. In fact, he seemed to be enjoying himself.

They put ten more levels behind them with no organized opposition. Hugh directed them not to kill peasants unnecessarily. The three bravoes obeyed; Bobo was too loaded down with Ertz to constitute a problem in discipline. Hugh saw to it that they put thirty-odd more decks below them and were well into no man's land before he let vigilance relax at all. Then he called a halt and they examined wounds.

The only deep ones were to Long Arm's arm and Bobo's face. Joe-Jim examined them and applied presses with which he had outfitted himself before starting. Hugh refused treatment for his flesh wound. "It's stopped bleeding," he insisted, "and I've got a lot to do."

"You've got nothing to do but to get up home," said Joe, "and that will be an end to this foolishness."

"Not quite," denied Hugh. "You may be going home, but Alan and I and Bobo are going up to no-weight—to the Captain's veranda."

"Nonsense," said Joe. "What for?"

"Come along if you like, and see. All right, gang. Let's go."

Joe started to speak, stopped when Jim kept still. Joe-Jim followed along.

They floated gently through the door of the veranda, Hugh, Alan, Bobo with his still-passive burden—and Joe-Jim. "That's it," said Hugh to Alan, waving his hand at the splendid stars, "that's what I've been telling you about."

Alan looked and clutched at Hugh's arm. "Jordan!" he moaned. "We'll fall out!" He closed his eyes tightly.

Hugh shook him. "It's all right," he said. "It's grand. Open your eyes."

Joe-Jim touched Hugh's arm. "What's it all about?" he demanded. "Why did you bring *him* up here?" He pointed to Ertz.

"Oh—him. Well, when he wakes up I'm going to show him the stars, prove to him that the Ship moves."

"Well? What for?"

"Then I'll send him back down to convince some others."

"Hm-m-m—suppose he doesn't have any better luck than you had?"

"Why, then"—Hugh shrugged his shoulders—"why, then we shall just have to do it all over, I suppose, till we do convince them.

"We've got to do it, you know."